Have a Highland Fling with
M. C. Beaton's

HAMISH MACBETH MYSTERIES

"It's always a special treat to return to Lochdubh."
—Marilyn Stasio, *New York Times Book Review*

"Reading Beaton is an experience akin to discovering buried treasure...An outstanding read from one of the real masters of mystery."
—*Booklist* (starred review)

"Macbeth's charm continues to grow...Fun, silly, and as light as a well-made scone—I wouldn't miss a single book."
—*Christian Science Monitor*

"The detective novels of M.C. Beaton, a master of outrageous black comedy...have reached cult status in the United States."
—*The Times Magazine* (London)

"Inspired...satisfying fun...Hamish is a gem."
—*Kirkus Reviews*

Death *of a* Travelling Man

Previous Hamish Macbeth Mysteries by M. C. Beaton

M. C. BEATON

Death *of a* Travelling Man

GRAND CENTRAL
PUBLISHING

NEW YORK   BOSTON

Copyright © 1993, 2009 by Marion Chesney
Excerpt from *Death of Yesterday* copyright © 2013 by Marion Chesney
Excerpt from *Death of an Outsider* copyright © 2012 by Marion Chesney
Excerpt from *Death of a Kingfisher* copyright © 2012 by Marion Chesney

Grand Central Publishing
Hachette Book Group
237 Park Avenue
New York, NY 10017
www.HachetteBookGroup.com

Grand Central Publishing is a division of Hachette Book Group, Inc.
The Grand Central Publishing name and logo is a trademark of Hachette Book Group, Inc.

The Hachette Speakers Bureau provides a wide range of authors for speaking events. To find out more, go to www.hachettespeakersbureau.com or call (866) 376-6591.

The publisher is not responsible for websites (or their content) that are not owned by the publisher.

Printed in the United States of America

First Grand Central Publishing mass market edition: April 2013

10 9 8 7 6 5 4 3 2 1
OPM

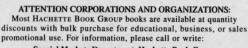

To Sacha Moore,
with love

Chapter One

From his brimstone bed, at break of day,
A-walking the Devil is gone,
To look at his little snug farm of the World,
And see how his stock went on.

—Robert Southey

Police Sergeant Hamish Macbeth was never to forget that fine spring day.

It was the day the devil came to Lochdubh.

Hamish was strolling along the waterfront of the tiny Highland village, glad to be free for a brief spell from the bloodhound efficiency of his sidekick, P.C. Willie Lamont. Although his promotion to sergeant had meant more pay, it had also meant that this eager beaver of a policeman had been thrust upon him, interfering with Hamish's easygoing life and home. Willie was also a cleanliness fanatic and Hamish was tired of living with the all-pervading smell of disinfectant.

The day was fine and warm, unusual for March in the Highlands. Snow glittered on the twin peaks of the mountains which soared above the village, and the sea loch lay calm and placid in the morning sun. Peat smoke rose from cottage chimneys, seagulls swooped and dived.

And then Hamish saw it, parked in front of what was once the Lochdubh Hotel, still up for sale. It was a battered old bus which had been converted into a travelling home. At one time in its career the bus had been painted psychedelic colours but even these had faded into pastel streaks overlaid with brown trails of rust.

Hamish went up to it and knocked at the door. The door jerked open. A tall man smiled down at Hamish. He was incredibly handsome. Jet black hair grew to a widow's peak on his forehead. His eyes were green, grass-green without a fleck of brown in them. His face and arms were tanned golden-brown. He was wearing a blue-and-white-checked shirt and blue jeans moulded to long muscular legs.

"You are not allowed to park here," said Hamish, wondering why he should take such an instant and violent dislike to this handsome man.

"I am a traveller," the man said in a cultivated English voice. "My name is Sean Gourlay."

Hamish's face hardened. Sean would have been called a hippie not so long ago and a beatnik a long time before that. Now he belonged to that unlovable crowd who euphemistically referred to themselves as travellers, the itinerant race who descended on places like Stonehenge complete with battered unlicensed vehicles, dirt, drugs and dogs. To some charitable souls who had never had their sheep ripped apart by dogs or their land turned into a sewer, the travellers carried with them an aura of romance, like the gypsies they pretended to be. Living on the dole, they travelled aimlessly from place to place. The reason these nomadic layabouts claimed to be "travellers" or sometimes "new travellers" was that they demanded the privileges and camping rights given to gypsies, privileges often dating back centuries. Hamish was tolerant of gypsies and knew them all. He had no time for these so-called travellers.

"You are not a gypsy," said Hamish, "and therefore have no rights. This is private property."

A girl squeezed in beside Sean at the doorway. She had straggly sun-bleached hair, a small dirty face, and a thin, flat-chested body.

"Get lost, pig," she said, in the guttural accents of Glasgow.

Hamish ignored her. He addressed himself to Sean. "I can direct you to a place up on the moors where you can camp."

Sean gave him a blinding smile. "But I like this village," he said.

"And so do I," retorted Hamish, "which is why I am ordering you to move on. Let's see your driving license."

A stream of four-letter words erupted from the girl. Sean dug into the back pocket of his jeans and produced a clean new driving license, issued only a few months ago. The girl had now jumped down from the bus. She was very small in stature. She leaped up and down in front of Hamish, cursing and yelling. "Pig" was the politest epithet. There was a peculiar, almost sinister magnetism about Sean. He paid no attention to the girl whatsoever and Hamish found himself doing the same. He examined Sean's insurance and the road-tax disc on the bus. Both were in order.

He handed back the papers and said firmly, "Now, get moving."

Sean grinned. "Certainly, officer."

The girl told Hamish to perform an impossible anatomical act on himself and then suddenly bolted back into the bus, like some small hairy animal darting into its lair.

"Pay no attention to Cheryl," said Sean lazily. "Rather an excitable type."

"Her full name?" snapped Hamish.

"Cheryl Higgins, like the professor."

Hamish waited until Sean had climbed into the driver's seat, until the bus clattered off. He stood with his hands on his hips and watched it go. Then he shook his head. He should not have allowed Sean to upset him. If they parked up on the moors, they would not stay long. He knew the travellers preferred to be with their own kind. It was unusual to find just two of them and one old bus. This fine weather was unusual. Soon there would be the "lambing blizzard," that last vicious fall of snow which always arrived in the late spring to plague the shepherds.

His mind turned to the problem of P.C. Willie Lamont. He would not have minded at all having a helper. All policemen, however crime-free the area they lived in, were landed with a lot of paperwork. Hamish regarded the police station as his home, his own home, and he wished he could manage to get Willie to live somewhere else in the village. As he ambled back again in the direction of the police station, he saw that his dog, Towser, was once more tied up in the garden. Poor Towser was always being banished outside these days, thought Hamish. Willie must be scrubbing the floors...again. He decided to go up to Tommel Castle Hotel where his friend, Priscilla Halburton-Smythe, was working in the hotel gift shop. Priscilla's father, Colonel Halburton-Smythe, had turned his home into a hotel to recoup the vast losses he had made by trusting his money to a charlatan. The hotel had prospered, having excellent shooting and fishing and high-enough charges to appeal to the snobbish and the parvenues who thought the colonel's high-handed manner with his guests was a sign of true breeding, rather than the mixture of arrogance and sheer bloody-mindedness that it, in truth, was.

As he unhitched Towser and led the dog to the police

Land Rover, Hamish reflected sadly that having Willie in the police station was like being married to a nag of a wife. Archie Maclean, the fisherman, spent most of his time either in the pub or sitting on the harbour wall to get away from his wife's perpetual cleaning.

The new gift shop was a pleasant place, full of the very best of Scottish goods: Edinburgh crystal, Caithness glass, silver jewellery, fine woollens, along with a multitude of cheaper goods for the tourist to take home—shortbread, locally made fudge, guidebooks, postcards, souvenir pens and pencils, and stuffed toys.

Priscilla was wearing her new tourist uniform of frilled white shirt and short tartan skirt. Hamish wondered what the tourists made of her, this graceful woman with the smooth blonde hair and the superb figure who looked as if she had stepped out of the pages of *Vogue*.

She saw Hamish and smiled. "I've had a coffee machine put in here. You must have got word of it."

"I am not mooching," said Hamish, who nearly always was. "But I will have the coffee, nonetheless."

"What brings you here, Sergeant?" asked Priscilla as she poured two mugs of coffee. She never tired of calling him Sergeant these days, he reflected. He knew she took his promotion as a sign that he had finally come to his senses and decided to be ambitious.

"It's Willie," he said. "Cleaning again. I cannae call my house my own."

"You're too easygoing, Hamish," said Priscilla

firmly. "You should put your foot down. Find him something to do."

"Well, I was thinking of phoning the superintendent and pointing out that there is not the work here for two men."

"And then what would happen?" demanded Priscilla. "The police station would be closed down and you would be moved to Strathbane and you would hate that. I mean, it's not as if you want to be demoted, is it?"

"As a matter o' fact that waud suit me chust fine," said Hamish, whose Highland accent became more marked when he was upset. "I had the good life afore the last murder and I should ha' let Blair take the credit for solving it." Detective Chief Inspector Blair was the bane of Hamish's life, but in the past he had let him take the credit for solving cases, not wanting any promotion to disturb his calm life. But at the end of the last case, during which Blair had been more than usually obnoxious, Hamish had cracked and told the superintendent that he had solved the case himself and so the result had been promotion to sergeant—and the arrival of Willie.

"Oh, Hamish, you're just saying that."

"No, I am not. I had the fine life afore I got these wretched stripes. I want Willie and his scrubbing brush out and I don't know how tae go about it."

She sat down on a high stool behind the counter and crossed her legs. They were excellent legs, thought Hamish not for the first time, but he wasn't going to be daft enough to fall in love with her again. He had enough trouble in his life with Willie.

"Look," said Priscilla, "here's something we could do."

Hamish brightened at the sound of that "we." He found another stool and perched on it, facing her over the glass counter. There was a sample bottle of a scent called Mist o' the Highlands. He sprayed some on his hand and sniffed it. It was very strong and very sweet and cloying.

"Pooh," he said, scrubbing at his hand.

"Can't you leave any free sample alone?" said Priscilla. "You'll smell of that stuff for weeks. Believe me, I've tried it. It's immune to soap and water. Now about Willie. He's a bachelor, right?"

"Aye, and likely to remain so," said Hamish with feeling. "What woman can compete with all thon cleaning and polishing and cooking? Besides, he's a terribly finicky eater."

"That doesn't matter. An awful lot of people are finicky eaters, and there are a lot of women who would be delighted to have a housekeeper."

"What are you getting at?"

"Find him a wife," said Priscilla. "If he gets married, there's no room in that station for a married couple. They'd need to find him new quarters."

Hamish's face brightened. Then it fell. "Who is there who would even look at the beast?"

"We've got a new hotel receptionist. Doris Ward's her name. Prissy, fussy, competent, not all that good-looking. Invite Willie up to the castle tonight and we'll all have dinner. It'll start his meeting females anyway."

"All right," said Hamish. "I'll try anything."

He was driving back slowly through the village but he slowed to a mere crawl as he saw a vision standing outside Napoli, the new Italian restaurant. The vision was shaking out a duster. She had an old-fashioned figure, that is, she had a voluptuous bust, a tiny waist and a saucy plump backside. She was wearing a short, skimpy black dress over which was tied a frilly checked apron. She had a heart-shaped face, a tiny nose and a wide soft mouth. Her hair was a riot of dusky curls. She was wearing very high heels and she had firm-muscled calves, like you see on dancer's legs.

Must be one of old Ferrari's relatives, thought Hamish. Mr. Ferrari was a Scottish Italian, that is, his father had settled in Scotland at the turn of the century. From his father, Mr. Ferrari had inherited a prosperous restaurant in Edinburgh, but having retired and turned it over to his sons, he found time lying heavy on his hands. And so he had started the restaurant in Lochdubh and staffed it with remoter relatives from Italy.

Hamish arrived at the police station in time to meet Willie, who had his uniform on and was preparing to leave.

"Where are you off to?" asked Hamish.

"There's gypsies up on the field at the back o' the manse," said Willie.

Hamish's eyes narrowed. "An old bus?"

"Aye."

"I'll come with you. They're not gypsies but travellers."

"Commercial travellers, sir?"

"No, I'll tell you about them as we go along."

Sure enough, there was the bus in the grassy field behind the manse.

Followed by Willie, Hamish knocked at the door. Cheryl opened it. "Two pigs," she said in disgust.

"Here now," said Willie, "there is no reason at all, at all to be using nasty words."

"Go screw," said Cheryl, and then, suddenly, she covered her face with her hands and began to sob pathetically, saying between her sobs, "Why are you always persecuting me?"

"And just what do you think you are doing, Sergeant?" demanded a wrathful voice from behind Hamish. He swung round. Mrs. Wellington, the minister's wife, stood there, and behind her was Sean, rocking lightly on his heels, a mocking look in his green eyes.

"I am moving these people on," said Hamish.

"You have no right to do any such thing," said Mrs. Wellington wrathfully. "I gave this young man permission to put his bus here, and that is all there is to it. These poor young people are hounded from pillar to post by bureaucratic monsters like yourself, Hamish Macbeth. These people of the road should be admired for their life-style."

"If you have given your permission," said Hamish, "then that is all right. But I shall be calling on you later."

As he walked off with Willie, he heard behind him Sean's light, amused laugh. "Get on to Strathbane," said Hamish to Willie, "and see if they have anything on their files on Sean Gourlay and Cheryl Higgins."

"Herself was a bit dirty-mouthed," said Willie, "but he seemed nice enough."

"He's as bad as she is and I have the feeling that he's dangerous."

"Well, now, sir, I am in the way of being a student o' human nature," said Willie. "I took a corresponding course in the psychotry."

"A correspondence course in psychiatry," corrected Hamish, who always felt he was fighting a losing battle against Willie's mistakes and malapropisms.

"Didn't I just say that?" demanded Willie, aggrieved. "Well, I would say from my experience that Sean Gourlay is just a regular, normal fellow."

"Never mind. Check up on him anyway," said Hamish. "And by the way, we're invited up to the castle for dinner tonight by Miss Halburton-Smythe."

"But we cannae dae that, sir," said Willie patiently. "That waud mean two of us off duty."

"We leave a note on the door o' the police station to say where we are," said Hamish, striving for patience. "What's going to happen in Lochdubh? The same as all the nights since you've been here . . . nothing at all."

"Well, I suppose..." Willie's voice trailed away and his mouth fell open. They had arrived outside the Italian restaurant and the beauty Hamish had seen earlier was down on her knees scrubbing the restaurant steps, her bottom waggling provocatively with each movement of the scrubbing brush. "That's something you dinnae say these days," said Willie, staring in admiration.

"What? A bum like that?" asked Hamish.

"No, a woman down on her knees scrubbing. I thought they were exstinked."

"Nice day," said Hamish loudly, raising his cap. The girl turned and looked up and then got to her feet, wiping her soapy hands on her apron.

"Just arrived?" pursued Hamish.

"Yes. Mr. Ferrari send for me last month."

"But you knew English already?"

"My mother, she is from Edinburgh. She go back to the village to get married. The village is outside Naples."

She held out a small work-reddened hand.

"I am Sergeant Hamish Macbeth and this is P.C. Willie Lamont," said Hamish, "and you are...?"

"Lucia Livia."

"And what do you think of Lochdubh, Miss Livia?"

"It is...very quiet," she said, her eyes looking beyond them to the still loch.

A group of fishermen and forestry workers came along and stopped short, all of them staring at Lucia in silent admiration.

"I feel it is the duty o' the police tae look after new-comers to the village," said Willie suddenly. "Perhaps you waud allow me to show you around the place, Miss Livia?"

"I am not sure," she said cautiously. "I would have to ask Mr. Ferrari. I work every evening."

"Aye, well, just you ask him," said Willie. "You've left the corners o' the steps dirty. That'll no' do. Wait and I'll show ye."

"For heffen's sake," muttered Hamish, his Highland accent becoming more sibilant. But Willie was already down on his knees, scrubbing busily at the step.

"I'll say good day to you, Miss Livia," said Hamish stiffly. "Some of us haff the police work to do."

Willie scrubbed on, unheeding.

Hamish walked gloomily back to the police station. In the small kitchen, everything gleamed and shone and the air smelled strongly of bleach and disinfectant. He made a cup of coffee and carried it through to the police station and sat down at the desk. He phoned Strathbane and spoke to Detective Jimmy Anderson, giving him the names of Cheryl and Sean. The address on Sean's driving license had been a Glasgow one and Hamish remembered it clearly, Flat B, 189, Lombard Crescent. Anderson said he would check up on it and get back to him as soon as possible.

Hamish then went out again and along to the manse. The minister was alone in his study. "Oh, Hamish," he said, pushing away the sermon he had been working on, "what brings you here?"

"It's those layabouts and their bus."

"They are doing no harm, Hamish. The field is not used for anything. It's a small patch of weedy grass and nettles. Why shouldn't these young people have the use of it?"

"There's something about them I don't like. Besides, I'm surprised at you, Mr. Wellington, for encouraging that kind of layabout."

"Now, Hamish," said the minister mildly, "you know jobs are few and far between."

"So why don't they go somewhere where there *are* jobs?" demanded Hamish, exasperated.

The minister chewed the end of his pencil in an abstracted way and then put it down. "There is something appealing about their way of life," he said. "I sometimes think it would be wonderful to just take off and travel around without any responsibilities whatsoever."

"And then who would pay the taxes?"

"They're both young," said Mr. Wellington comfortably. "Time enough yet for them to grow up and become responsible."

"Sean Gourlay is, I should guess, in his late twenties," pointed out Hamish, "and the girl has a gutter mouth."

"Come now, she was charming to me."

"Well, I feel you are being conned," said Hamish. "Don't say I didn't warn you!"

*   *   *

Hamish and Willie drove up to Tommel Castle Hotel that evening. Hamish climbed down from the Land Rover and sniffed the soft air with pleasure. The light evenings were back. Gone was the long dark tunnel of winter. A faint breeze blew in from the moors, scented with wild thyme. And then one of the castle cars, driven by a young woman, drove up and began to reverse to park next to the police Land Rover.

"Wait a minute," shouted Willie, moving purposefully forward. "You're no' doing it right. Hard left. Now straighten up! Straighten up. Dear God, lassie, how did you ever pass your test? Don't you know how to straighten up?"

Face scarlet with a mixture of fury and mortification, the woman parked at an angle and then climbed out and slammed the car door.

Willie shook his head. "Women drivers," he said. "You'll need to do better than that."

She gave him an angry look and walked off into the hotel without a word.

"Stop being Mr. Know-All," said Hamish. "She'd probably haff done chust fine if you had left her alone. Now forget you're a cop, and try to be charming."

Suddenly nervous, Willie tugged at his tie. "Do I look all right, sir?"

"Yes, yes, just watch that mouth of yours."

Priscilla met them in the entrance hall. "Doris is

waiting for us in the bar," she said. "I told her to get herself a drink and settle down. Some fool of a man was trying to tell her how to park."

Hamish groaned inwardly. Doris Ward was a plain young woman with thick glasses and a rather rabbity mouth. She was wearing a blouse and skirt and a tartan waistcoat. She shook hands with Willie and Hamish and then said to Willie, "I should have known you were a bobby."

"Sorry about that," said Willie awkwardly after a nudge in the ribs from Hamish's elbow. "Forgot I was off duty."

"I am sure you have more to do when you are *on* duty," said Doris, "than hector women drivers."

"You're English, aren't you?" said Hamish, desperate to change the conversation. "Thanks, Priscilla, I'll have any sort of soft drink, but Willie here will have a whisky."

"Yes, I'm English," said Doris. "It's all very remote up here, isn't it?"

Everyone agreed that, yes, it was remote and then there was a heavy silence.

"Willie here is from the city, Strathbane," said Hamish at last. "He's finding it difficult to get used to village ways."

"Do you have many friends in the village?" Doris asked Willie politely.

"No, not in Lochdubh," said Willie, "but I have a cliché of friends in Strathbane."

"Clique," moaned Hamish under his breath.

"Mind you," said Willie, becoming expansive, "I have always wanted to travel. I have an aunt in America I could go and see."

"Which part of America?" asked Doris.

"She lives in a condom in San Francisco."

Doris sniggered. "Well, in these AIDS-ridden days, that's a very safe place to live."

Willie looked at her, puzzled, and then his face cleared. "Oh, aye, them condoms have secured cameras and guards and things like that."

"Do you want to travel yourself, Doris?" asked Hamish.

"Oh, I don't know." Behind her thick glasses, her eyes sent him a flirtatious look. "I might settle for marriage."

"Quite right too," said Willie heartily. "I must say, it is refreshing to meet the woman these days who disnae go in for all this fenimist rubbish."

"You mean *feminist*," corrected Doris. "If you are going to criticize anything, at least pronounce it properly. Do you mean all women should settle for marriage and babies?"

"Why not?" demanded Willie, giving her a tolerant smile. "That's what they're built for."

"You're out of the Dark Ages," said Priscilla smoothly. "Dinner should be ready now. Carry your drinks through."

"Get her to talk about herself," hissed Hamish in Willie's ear as they walked towards the dining-room.

But no sooner were they seated and waiting for the first course to be served than Doris selected a cigarette from a packet and lit up.

"Do you know you are ruining your lungs?" demanded Willie. "That stuff's a killer and bad for the skin, too. I can already see it has—"

"What are we haffing for dinner?" said Hamish, his voice suddenly very loud and strained.

"Scotch broth to start," said Priscilla, "and then steak. We've got a new chef. We had to get rid of the old one," she said to Doris, "after that murder here, the one I told you about."

Doris gazed at Hamish with admiration. "I heard you'd solved it," she said. "Tell me all about it."

Normally too shy to talk much about himself but frightened of Willie's gaffes, Hamish told her about it at length, but Priscilla saw to her irritation that Doris was entranced with Hamish and could hardly keep her eyes off him.

The evening went from bad to worse. Hamish had never before seen Willie drink anything stronger than tea or coffee. The whisky before dinner, the wine at dinner and the brandy afterwards went straight to his head. As soon as Hamish had finished talking, Willie began to talk about *his* cases, which sounded like a dismal catalogue of public harassment. He seemed a genius at finding out cars with bald tyres, cars with lapsed road tax, cars with various other faults, and every parking offence under the sun. He told what he obviously thought were hilarious stories of people who had become angry with him and what they had said. He laughed so hard, the tears ran down his face. Willie had never before enjoyed himself so much. He felt he was the life and soul of the party.

Hamish at last propelled a dreamily smiling Willie out to the Land Rover. "You made a fine mess o' that, Willie," he said as he drove down to Lochdubh through the heathery darkness. But there was no reply. Willie had fallen asleep.

What on earth am I going to do with him, thought Hamish wearily. Up on the field behind the manse, lights glowed behind the curtained windows of the bus. He did not like the sight. He did not like the feeling of this alien and dangerous presence in Lochdubh.

He then reassured himself with the thought that they would soon get bored and move on. The "travellers" like to journey in convoys. It was odd to find two of them on their own.

He woke Willie outside the police station and ordered him sharply to go in and go to bed. Then he phoned Strathbane. Jimmy Anderson was working overtime and took the call. He had, he said, found nothing on Cheryl and Sean Gourlay from the Glasgow police except to confirm that Sean had taken his driving test in Glasgow recently, hence the new license.

"Try Scotland Yard," urged Hamish. "See what they can come up with."

"Whit? They're overworked down there as it is," complained Anderson. "Whit's this Sean done?"

"Nothing . . . yet," said Hamish. "Look, just try them."

"Try them yoursel'," said Anderson. "We've got more than enough work here. In my opinion, you're going a bit ower the top about this Sean character. Wait till he does something."

Hamish put down the receiver. He felt he had been a bit silly. There was no need to phone the Yard.

Besides, what could he have told Scotland Yard anyway? That he had a bad feeling, an intuition?

Sean would be gone by next week at the latest. And with that comforting thought, Hamish went to bed.

Chapter Two

We believe no evil till the evil's done.

—Jean de la Fontaine

But a week later, the bus was still parked up behind the manse. A much cleaner and quieter Cheryl than Hamish had first met wandered about the village or up on the moors. She and Sean were hardly ever to be seen together. They seemed a popular-enough pair with the villagers, who were all Highland enough to admire really genuine laziness when they saw it, and Hamish was irritated to overhear one of the village women saying, "Thon Sean Gourlay can beat our Hamish any day when it comes to the idleness."

Hamish felt this was particularly unfair, as he had suddenly been beset with a series of small accidents and crimes to deal with. There were frying-pan fires, minor car crashes, lost sheep, lost children, boundary disputes, poachers, and various other things which seemed like dramas at the outset and resolved themselves into minor happenings at the end. Particularly the three reported cases of lost children, who turned out to have been playing truant from school to go fishing. But it still meant a lot of paperwork, and Hamish found that easier to do himself than to spend hours correcting Willie's prose.

The weather was still unseasonably mild and all the burns and rivers were foaming with peaty water, like beer, as they rushed down from the hills and mountains fed by melting snow. The air was full of the sound of rushing water. Curlews piped on the moors, sailing over their nests, their long curved beaks giving them a prehistoric look. There were vast skies of milky blue and tremendous sunsets of feathery pink clouds, long bands of them, each cloud as delicate as a brush-stroke.

Hamish would have put Sean Gourlay out of his mind had he not found him hanging around the hotel gift shop where Priscilla worked.

Sean gave Hamish his usual mocking look as he strolled out of the shop. Hamish waited until he had gone and then said to Priscilla, "You shouldn't encourage him."

"Why not?" demanded Priscilla coolly. "The first time he bought a silver-and-amethyst ring, and the second, a mohair shawl. He's a genuine customer, Hamish."

"Where does he get the money?" demanded Hamish. "I happen to know the pair o' them are drawing the dole from the post office."

"Maybe he's got a private income," said Priscilla. "Look, Hamish, the way you go on and on about layabouts is a joke. You've never been a one for hard work yourself."

"Aye, but I get my money honestly," said Hamish, annoyed that she should defend Sean.

"Hamish, I happen to know that you poach salmon from the river."

"Well, only the odd one."

"Still, that's stealing. You're supposed to stop poaching."

"It's the gangs that dynamite the rivers I'm after," said Hamish huffily. "I don't do any harm."

"You must have less than ever to do now that you've got Willie," pursued Priscilla.

"On the contrary, I've got double the work. That fellow *makes* work. That was a grand idea of yours to get him married off, but there isnae a woman in Lochdubh that would have him."

"Seen anything of Doris?" asked Priscilla casually.

"She called at the police station a couple of times, just in a friendly way," said Hamish defensively.

The phone on the wall rang shrilly and Priscilla picked it up. "It's for you," she said, handing the receiver to Hamish.

Mrs. Wellington's voice sounded shrill and harsh from the other end. "Hamish, wee Roderick Fairley is trapped on a rock in the Anstey below the bridge and the river's rising by the minute. Where were you? Why isn't there anyone at the police station? Why—?"

Hamish dropped the receiver on the counter. "There's a wee boy stuck on a rock in the Anstey," he said to Priscilla. "See if you can get Willie."

As he ran out, he could hear Mrs. Wellington's voice still squawking from the receiver.

He drove fast down to the village. He could see a group of men and women hanging over the parapet of the hump-backed bridge over the River Anstey.

He jumped down from the Land Rover and pushed them aside.

Roderick Fairley, a chubby five-year-old with hair as flaming red as Hamish's own, was sitting astride a large rock in the middle of the river, which was foaming about him with a deafening roar.

"The river's rising every minute," said a man at Hamish's ear. "We'd throw the wee lad a rope but the force o' that water'd pull his arms frae their sockets."

"Get a ladder," said Hamish. He scrabbled down the side of the bridge and onto the riverbank. The force of the water was tremendous as it cascaded under the bridge and poured around large rocks like the one on which the child was sitting and then hurtled down the falls below. Rainbows rose in the air above the water. Hamish cupped his hands to call to the boy and then realized that Roderick would not be able to hear him above the force of the river.

"Here's Jimmy with the ladder," came a voice, and Hamish twisted about. "Bring it here," he shouted, "and we'll lay it from the bank to the rock."

More faces peered over the parapet of the bridge. With the help of Jimmy Gordon, a forestry worker, Hamish laid the long ladder from the bank out to the rock. The terrified Roderick sat motionless, his mouth open in a soundless wail of fear.

"It's no' very steady," shouted Jimmy.

Hamish asked, "How did he get over there?"

"His friend says they was jumping frae rock tae rock and then the river rose sudden-like," said Jimmy.

More men had come up. "Now," said Hamish, removing his cap and throwing it down on the bank, "you lot hold the ladder steady."

Hamish began to inch his way across. A great silence fell on the watching crowd. The roar of the water seemed to be louder and stronger. He pulled himself along the ladder, shouting as he did so, "Don't be afraid, Roddy. I'm nearly there."

And then the roar of the water became louder, and high above it rose a great keening wail of distress from the women on the bridge and on the banks. Hamish cast one frightened agonized look up the river and saw a wall of water rushing down the mountain towards the bridge and made a lunge and grabbed the child just as the water struck with full force.

Priscilla arrived just in time to see the crowd scatter from the bridge before the torrent struck, to see Hamish's red hair disappearing under the roaring flood. Stumbling and cursing and weeping, she made her way down towards the loch, over boulders and roots of shaggy fir trees, over tearing brambles and down to the beach. Her eyes raked the torrential stream and then the waters of the loch. Nothing.

From all over the village, people were running to the beach.

Priscilla stopped at the edge of the loch and stood panting. Mrs. Fairley, the little boy's mother, was kneeling by the side of the water, crying out in Gaelic to the ancient gods to give her back her son.

And then the waters out in the loch broke and Hamish's head rose above them. He was holding the boy fast. He swam to shore while Priscilla and the others waded out into the loch to meet him.

"Quick," panted Hamish. "He may be alive yet."

The boy lay in his arms as still as death.

Hamish laid the boy facedown on the beach and then began to pump his little arms up and down. Suddenly, water gushed from the boy's mouth and he set up a wail.

"He's alive. Roddy's alive." The news spread out from the shoreline. Mrs. Fairley fainted dead away. Dr.

Brodie arrived with his medical bag and gently pushed Hamish aside. Hamish sat down on the beach and put his head in his hands.

"Hamish, Hamish, I thought you were dead," whispered Priscilla in his ear.

"Aye," said Hamish on a sigh. "I thought that myself."

"Did you get a battering on the rocks?"

"No, there was such a lot of water, it swept us over them. Where did it all come from?"

"The Drum Loch at the top got filled up wi' melting snow and burst its banks," said Archie Maclean, the fisherman. "I hivnae seen the like since '46."

An Air-Sea Rescue helicopter was landing a little way away along the beach. Hamish shivered. Dr. Brodie said, "He'll live. We'll get the helicopter to take him to hospital just to be sure. I'll attend to his mother and then she'd better go with him. You'd best go home and get a hot drink, Hamish. No broken bones?"

"No, I'm chust fine," said Hamish. Followed by Priscilla, he made his way through the crowd. People slapped him on the back and shook his hand as he passed.

"Where's Willie?" asked Hamish.

"I don't know," said Priscilla. "I certainly didn't see him anywhere about."

They had walked together along the beach away from the roaring, foaming river. They came to a flight of seaweedy stone steps cut into the sea-wall and climbed up them onto the waterfront. In front of them on the other side of the road was the Napoli restaurant, and there, at the side door of the restaurant, in the nonchalant manner of a stage-door Johnnie, was Willie.

"Willie!" shouted Hamish.

Willie started guiltily and then came running over, seemingly aware for the first time of the crowds, the helicopter and the dripping-wet Hamish. "Whit happened?" he asked.

"Hamish has just rescued a little boy from drowning," said Priscilla.

"And where were you?" demanded Hamish.

"I just called on that Miss Livia," said Willie and then blushed. "I wanted to see how she was getting on, it being part of my duties to look out for the welfare of the incomer."

"Your job," said Hamish wrathfully, "is to look out for the welfare of people in trouble. Get back to the station and sit by that phone in the office until I tell you to move. Hop to it!"

Willie sulkily touched his cap with one forefinger and then slouched off.

"He'll haff to go," said Hamish Macbeth.

The enterprising Mr. Patel, who owned the local supermarket, had grabbed the shop video camera, which he rented out for occasions like weddings and dances, and had filmed the whole of Hamish Macbeth's dramatic rescue. He had then driven at great speed all the way to the headquarters of Highland Television, where he had sold them the video. Detective Chief Inspector Blair, on his day off, and planning to relax in front of the news, had all the doubtful pleasure of watching Hamish Macbeth on television. Mr. Patel had done a good job. It was all there—from the striking of the wave and the disappearance of Hamish to his re-emergence in the loch. There was even a quote from Hamish. "At his police station in Lochdubh, Sergeant Hamish Macbeth said he was only doing his job." The quote had actually come from Willie, who had been told to say that to any of the press who phoned up.

Blair bit his thumb and scowled horribly at the television set. Something would have to be done about Macbeth or he would go on getting promoted until he rose up the ranks and became his, Blair's, boss. There must be some way of discrediting Hamish.

The next day brought one of those abrupt changes in the weather in Sutherland. The wind moved round to the northeast and a blizzard whitened the countryside, blocking the roads and cutting Lochdubh off from the rest of the world.

Harry Tennant, the garbage collector, who was supposed to operate the gritting truck and snow-plough in bad weather, celebrating the prospect of overtime, fell asleep at the wheel and overturned the truck into a ditch, and so the roads remained ungritted and unsalted. Hamish felt Tommel Castle Hotel might have been moved to Australia, for all the chance he had of reaching it and seeing Priscilla. His near drowning had had a profound effect on him. He felt his life had hitherto been drifting amiably along, and somehow he felt he should now do something to alter it. He had not travelled. There was a whole world beyond Lochdubh, Lochdubh where he was snowed up in a police station with Willie and Towser for company. He had given away his television set as a bribe during his last big case, and so there was nothing to lighten the gloom, for he had read all of Mr. Patel's small stock of paperbacks.

He went out into the driving snow to feed his hens and then shovelled a path to the gate, feeling as he did so that it was a sheer waste of time. The snow eased a little and as he looked along the waterfront, he could see a tall figure on skis heading out of the village. Sean. And Sean was surely going in the direction of Tommel Castle. He went back into the house and was strapping on his own skis to go in pursuit when Willie came through from the office. "There's two climbers up on the mountain by the Drum Loch. They're trapped up on a crag. Thon shepherd, Jamie Macfarlane's jist phoned in tae say he can jist see them but cannae get tae them."

"Have you phoned Mountain Rescue?"

"Not yet."

"Do it and then get on your skis."

"I havenae got any skis."

"There's a spare pair out in the shed."

"I cannae ski. There was nae need for sich activities in the town."

"Get on the phone then." Hamish stood up and strapped a pair of snow-shoes on his back and then slung a bag with an emergency medical kit over his shoulder.

Willie went rather sulkily back to the office.

Power's not a very good thing, thought Hamish ruefully, as he set out into the snow. Willie's a pain in the neck, but I always seem to be snapping at him.

Priscilla had just finished stock-taking. As usual, she had opened the shop, despite the weather, because the hotel was full and guests often dropped in for a chat or to buy something to take home.

The door of the shop swung open, letting in a whirling cloud of snow. Sean Gourlay stood there, grinning, pulling off a ski mask.

"What brings you here?" asked Priscilla. "It's hardly a day for shopping for souvenirs."

He stooped down and took off his skis. Then he removed his anorak and swung it over the back of a chair. "I thought I might get a cup of coffee and a chat," he said, smiling at her. "It's awfully boring with all this snow."

He had come close to her as he spoke. He was, thought Priscilla, not for the first time, a devastatingly handsome man. But there was Cheryl.

"How's your girlfriend coping with it all?" she asked, backing away and then turning round to pour him a cup of coffee.

"Oh, whining as usual," he said with a light laugh. He took the mug of coffee from her. "Cheryl's not really my girlfriend, just a little creature who tags along."

"Oh, really," said Priscilla coolly.

"I know that sounds cruel, but she had been living with this chap and he threw her out, so she had nowhere else to go. What does a beauty like you find to do in Peasantville?"

"Helping to run a family hotel keeps me very busy," said Priscilla. His very presence was making her feel claustrophobic. His grass-green eyes were glittering hypnotically and he was exuding a strong air of male virility.

"Never feel like running away from it all?"

"No. I like it here."

"And what about boyfriends?"

"Mind your own business."

He smiled at her, unruffled. "Can't be much around here," he said. "You don't fit in. You're much too glamorous for a place like this."

Priscilla gave an impatient little sigh. "Do you want to buy anything?"

"I might." His eyes roamed over the goods and then came to rest on Priscilla's coat and scarf, which were hanging on a hook behind the counter. "Perhaps that scarf."

"That's mine."

"I'd like to buy it, nonetheless. I'd like something of yours."

"Perhaps you had better go, Mr. Gourlay."

He came round the counter and stood next to her, very close. "No, I don't think so," he said softly. "Not until I get that scarf."

Priscilla backed off to the end of the counter and then she quickly pressed the alarm bell under it. Immediately she had done it, she felt silly. There was no need to feel so frightened of him. Men had made passes at her before.

"Finish your coffee and go," she said firmly. "You are wasting my time and I've got a job to do."

The shop door crashed open and Dougie the gamekeeper stood there, a shotgun in his hand. "I heard the bell," he said.

Priscilla now felt thoroughly foolish. "I must have pressed it by mistake. This is Mr. Gourlay, Dougie. He's just leaving."

Sean clipped on his skis and put on his coat. He pulled a black ski mask down over his face. " 'Bye, beautiful," he said. And then he was off.

"Did ye really press thon bell by accident?" asked Dougie.

"No," said Priscilla. "He scared me. I don't know why."

"If he comes again," said Dougie, "jist ring the bell. And tell Hamish about this."

"There's no need to tell Hamish," said Priscilla. "He's probably having a lovely time sitting in his kitchen with his feet on the stove."

Then she gave an exclamation. "My scarf's gone. He must have taken it."

"Aye, weel, ye'll need tae phone Hamish now. That's theft."

Sean skied easily down towards the village. He had heard gossip about the local bobby and Priscilla. Some said he was sweet on her, some said she was sweet on him. Whatever way, he planned to let Hamish see him wearing the scarf. Irritating that Highland pig would be a pleasure. And then he cursed under his breath. Who was to know whether Hamish would recognize that scarf? And what if that hoity-toity bitch called him to report a theft? Then Hamish would have him, Sean, just where he wanted him. Damn. He skied back and made his way across country so that he would arrive at the back of the shop. The snow was easing now. He looked in the window. Priscilla was just putting on her coat. Then she switched off the lights and went out and locked the shop door behind her.

He waited a few moments and then slid quietly

round to the front. He unzipped a pocket in his anorak and took out a set of tools. He fiddled expertly with the lock until the tumblers clicked and then he eased the door open. It only took a moment to go quickly in and drop the scarf on the floor behind the counter. Then, just as quickly, he was outside again and had locked the door.

Hamish Macbeth had finally managed to reach the stranded climbers. One man was all right, the other man's leg had been broken in several places. Hamish gave him an injection and then sent up a distress flare, hoping he himself would not die of exposure before the Mountain Rescue team found them. He was too weary to give these inexperienced climbers a lecture on the folly of going up mountains in the north of Scotland in such weather. At least the snow was thinning slightly, but it was bitter cold.

To his relief, he heard the whirring of helicopter blades and stood up and waved and shouted. One by one, they were hoisted into the helicopter, the injured man, strapped onto a stretcher, going first. "Set me down in the village," shouted Hamish above the roar of the engine and the pilot nodded.

How incredibly long it had taken to climb up the mountain to that crag and how quickly he was whizzed down and deposited on the waterfront in front of the wide car-park of the deserted Lochdubh Hotel. He trudged wearily along to the police station, aching in every muscle.

He was furious to find the station unmanned and the kitchen stove out. But perhaps Willie had been called out on an emergency. He played back the answering service and heard Priscilla's voice asking him to call.

He sat down and phoned her at the hotel and listened to the tale of the theft of the scarf. As he spoke to her, a churning, grating and whirring sound from outside told him that the Lochdubh snow-plough was once more back in action.

"Don't worry, Priscilla," said Hamish. "In a way that's the best news I've heard all day. I'll get rid of the bastard now."

He left a note for Willie and then got out the Land Rover and moved off slowly along the newly cleared road. He stopped at the manse. The lights were on in the front room and he could clearly see Sean sitting at the dining table with the minister and his wife. There was no sign of Cheryl.

Well, he thought with satisfaction, what'll they think of their ewe lamb when they hear what I've got to say?

Mrs. Wellington answered the door and looked with disfavour at the tall lanky figure of the sergeant.

"What is it, Hamish?"

"I want a word with Sean Gourlay."

"Come in."

Hamish followed her into the manse dining-room. "Sean Gourlay," said Hamish, "I am arresting you for theft and must ask you to accompany me to the police station. Anything you say—"

"Wait a minute," said Sean easily. "Theft of what?"

"Miss Halburton-Smythe's scarf. You took it from her gift shop this afternoon."

"This is ridiculous," exclaimed Mrs. Wellington. "She probably lost it."

"It's an awful fuss to make about a scarf," pointed out the minister. "My umbrella was stolen last time I was in the Lochdubh bar, but no one did anything about that."

"Nonetheless," began Hamish, "I—"

"Fiddlesticks!" said Mrs. Wellington. "We are going up right now to have a look at that gift shop, and mark my words, I am sure that scarf will be there. Young girls are so careless."

"If you insist," said Hamish. "I can take a statement from Priscilla when I'm there."

He drove them up to the castle and received a long lecture from Mrs. Wellington about how police were always persecuting innocent citizens instead of going after real criminals.

Priscilla avoided looking at Sean as she led them all over to the gift shop and unlocked the door and switched on the lights. "My scarf was with my coat on that hook behind the counter," said Priscilla. "Mr. Gourlay said he wanted it."

"Why?" asked Hamish sharply.

"It's a pretty one and I thought poor little Cheryl might like that."

"That's not what you said to me," protested Priscilla.

"This is all a fuss about nothing." Mrs. Wellington heaved her tweedy bulk behind the counter. "You probably dropped that scarf. It's probably on the floor or somewhere. Why, here it is!" She held it up. "Is this the scarf?"

"Yes," said Priscilla, amazed. "But how...?"

"How did it get there?" demanded Mrs. Wellington. "It didn't *get* anywhere. It just lay where you dropped it while you and this Highland layabout go around persecuting innocent young men. Oh, yes, Hamish, I know you've had your knife into poor Sean since the day he arrived."

Her booming voice went remorselessly on and on while Hamish led them out to the car. She was still berating him when he dropped them off at the manse. "And furthermore," added Mrs. Wellington, "Miss Halburton-Smythe is being influenced by your tawdry mind. She is a lady. I know we are supposed to live in a classless society, but you would do better, Hamish Macbeth, to consort with your own kind of female!" Sean let out a chuckle of sheer delight.

Exhausted and furious, Hamish headed for home

and then slammed on the brakes outside the Napoli restaurant. In the glow of candle-light he could see Willie seated at a window table.

He hurtled into the restaurant and towered over Willie, who cringed when he saw him.

"What the devil do you think you are doing?" howled Hamish.

Lucia rushed forward, her eyes full of tears. "He was helping me," she sobbed.

"Now then." Old Mr. Ferrari made his majestic way over. "Haud yer wheest, Sergeant. The policeman here was helping Lucia clean the stove in the kitchen, and a grand job he made o' it, too. If all the coppers in Scotland were that helpful, the polis might hae a better image."

Hamish sank down suddenly into the chair opposite Willie. "Has everyone run mad?" he asked. "Begin at the beginning, Willie, and tell me why you left your post."

"It was awf'y quiet," said Willie, "and I thocht I'd jist call at the kitchen door to see if Lucia was all right. You see, I think it's part o' ma duties tae—"

"Yes, yes," said Hamish. "Skip that bit."

"Well, herself was scrubbing at the stove wi' her wee hands and no' doin' the job well at all, at all. 'You need pure ammonia for that,' I says and I hae a bottle at the station. I only meant tae show her, but I got working and I didnae notice the time and then Mr. Ferrari told me tae sit down and hae a glass o' wine. So I was jist having a glass o' chanter when you walked in."

"Chianti," said Hamish.

"Aye, weel, that's what I said."

Hamish leaned back in his chair and surveyed his side-kick and took several deep breaths. If Willie had not been in Lochdubh, he thought, then his own day would have been much the same. Perhaps instead of constantly shouting at this infuriating policeman, it might be an idea to try some kindness.

"Some wine?" asked Mr. Ferrari, deftly placing a glass in front of Hamish with one hand and holding up a bottle with the other.

Hamish Macbeth sighed. If you can't beat them, join them.

"Aye, that would be grand," he said.

Chapter Three

"I'll hae the law on ye, ye randy! I'll hae yer life!"

—S. R. Crockett

A hard frost set in, turning Lochdubh into a Christmas card, and slowing the tumult of the River Anstey.

A subdued Willie told Hamish, when the sergeant had returned from an early-morning walk around the village, that headquarters at Strathbane had called and that he was to phone Superintendent Peter Daviot immediately.

Puzzled, Hamish phoned. The superintendent was not available but his secretary said the message was that he was to report to Strathbane in person as soon as possible, but she could not say what it was about.

"They're probably going to give you some sort o' medal," said Willie, "for the wee laddie's rescue."

"Maybe," said Hamish, fighting down a feeling of unease, "although I thought if that was the case they might have sent me a formal letter. Keep the house warm,

Willie, and I'll talk to that scunner Blair again about the central heating he promised me and didn't deliver. Check the sheep-dip papers and don't forget to cover the beat. The roads are terrible and someone could be in trouble. Use your own car. I'll need to take the Land Rover with me. I've forgotten to give the sheep their winter feed. Do that and make sure they've got water."

"Hardly the job for a policeman," mumbled Willie, who seemed determined to remain in a prolonged sulk.

No sooner had Hamish driven off than Willie darted into the office and phoned a friend at headquarters and asked why Hamish was being sent for.

"Oh, it's a right goings-on," said the friend. "Some tart's come in, screaming fur the super and carrying a baby. She says the bairn's father is Hamish Macbeth."

"Oh, my!" exclaimed Willie in simple delight.

"He's goin' tae have that uniform and stripes ripped off him," said the friend. "I should think the police station at Lochdubh will be yours after today."

Willie thanked him and put down the phone. He went through to the living quarters and looked slowly around. He could get that wallpaper with the nice Regency stripe for the living-room and get rid of that nasty open fire which caused so much dust and put in one of those electric ones with the fake logs. He would take over Hamish's bedroom, which was larger than his own. He would rip the wood-burning stove out of the kitchen and replace it with a Calor gas cooker. He rubbed his hands gleefully. And that battered armchair Hamish liked so much could go for a start. A good spring cleaning was what the place needed. Whistling cheerfully, he tied on an apron and got to work.

Hamish sat nervously in the superintendent's office in Strathbane Police Headquarters. Strathbane! How he hated the place. A dreary, soulless town on the edge of the sea, with rotting docks and rotten houses and a general grey air of failure.

Superintendent Peter Daviot came in and Hamish jumped to his feet.

"Sit down, Macbeth," said the superintendent. No "Hamish." A bad sign.

"What's it about?" asked Hamish, wondering if Priscilla's father's water bailiff had seen him poaching on the river and reported him.

"It's about Maggie Dunlop."

"Who?"

"Come, come, Sergeant, let's talk this out man to man. Maggie Dunlop is waiting downstairs with your son."

"My—! This is a bad joke."

"No, Macbeth, she has reliable witnesses and photographs to prove it."

Hamish leaned back in his chair and said very quietly, "Let's have the lassie in here. I'm fascinated."

"Very well. I'm sorry about this. I thought you were doing so well, and the rescue of that little boy from the river was a credit to the force." He pressed a bell on his desk and said, "Send up Miss Dunlop. You will find her with Mr. Blair."

"Blair," said Hamish slowly. "Is he behind this?"

"I don't know what you mean. He happened to be here when she called—in great distress, I may add."

After a few moments the door opened and Blair ushered in a scrawny girl clutching a dirty baby. "Oh, Hamish," she cried when she saw him. "How could ye?"

"I've never seen you before in my life," said Hamish flatly.

She began to weep and wail while the baby bawled. Blair thrust two photographs at Hamish. "Whit hae ye tae say tae that, laddie?"

Hamish stared down at the photographs in bewilderment. They were two snapshots of him with Maggie. He was smiling and had an arm around her shoulders. In each photo he was in uniform. "They must be fakes," he said.

The baby abruptly stopped crying and looked at Hamish wide-eyed.

Mr. Daviot leaned forward and clasped his hands. "Now we all make mistakes. This happened three years ago, Miss Dunlop says. She says she's written to you several times begging for support money for the child, but you never answered."

"And who is this reliable witness or witnesses?" demanded Hamish grimly.

"Mr. and Mrs. John Tullyfeather, who live next door to Maggie, can testify that you visited her frequently."

"And where do they and this woman here live?"

"The Nelson Mandela block of flats down by the old dock. Stop this farce, Hamish. As you very well know, Miss Dunlop lives at number 23."

Blair gave a coarse laugh. "Ye cannae get yer leg over these days, Hamish, withoot paying the consequences."

"That's quite enough of that," snapped Mr. Daviot. "You may get back to your duties, Blair."

Blair left reluctantly.

Hamish looked closely at the photographs again. He suddenly remembered the horrible time when the police station had been closed down in Lochdubh and he had been called to serve on the force in Strathbane. Before his blessed return to his village, where the locals had organized a crime wave to get him back, he had had his photograph taken down on the waterfront by Jimmy Anderson. But in those pictures he had been standing with his arm around W.P.C. Pat Macleod. Jimmy had given him the film to get developed, but then Hamish had had the glad news of his return and had left the roll of film in his desk. So someone, probably Blair, had got the film and persuaded some bent photographer, probably himself—Hamish remembered the detective saying he had a dark-room at home—to fake up the photos.

"Could I haff a word with you in private, sir," said Hamish.

"Indeed you can. This ugly business must be cleared up," said Mr. Daviot. "Goodness, if the local press got their hands on this!" He rang the bell and told his secretary to take Miss Dunlop to the canteen and see that she had tea and cakes.

Maggie Dunlop left, strangely silent, but eyeing Hamish uneasily as she went.

Hamish tapped the photographs. "If you ask Jimmy Anderson, he will remember taking photos of me with Policewoman Macleod in that location. Someone has found the film, taken photos of this Maggie and faked them."

"Who would do such a thing?"

"Someone who didn't like me being made sergeant or getting all that coverage on television?"

"If you mean a jealous member of the police force, you must be mistaken! You may as well tell the truth."

"Furthermore, sir," said Hamish quietly, "did you check whether this Maggie Dunlop and the reliable witnesses have criminal backgrounds?"

"Of course not. Why?"

"Chust do me a favour," said Hamish, "and ask. My job's on the line."

"Oh, very well." Mr. Daviot picked up the phone and

rapped the necessary instructions down it. Hamish leaned back in his chair and folded his arms. "We'll chust wait and see."

It seemed an age before the phone rang. Mr. Daviot snatched it up and listened intently. Then he gazed at Hamish as the voice went on, his eyes round.

He finally put the phone down and said awkwardly, "Well, Hamish, it seems as if you have the right of it. I asked Pat Macleod to check and there was nothing on our files against either of them, but she's a bright girl and she checked the Central Scottish Criminal Records by phone. Maggie Dunlop, or certainly a Maggie Dunlop who fits the description of your accuser, was a well-known prostitute in Glasgow. She became pregnant and decided to start a new life up here. James Tullyfeather is also from Glasgow and has just finished doing ten years for armed robbery. There can't be more than one robber with a name like Tullyfeather. This is terrible. Who would do such a thing to you? Wait here." He shot out the door.

So, thought Hamish, beginning to relax. Blair's up to his tricks. If Maggie Dunlop's still in the canteen, I'm a Dutchman. Blair would be hanging about to find out what was going on and he'd know Pat was checking up. He must nearly have had a heart attack when she moved over to checking the Central Criminal Records.

After a long time, the superintendent came back and slumped down heavily into his chair. "What a mess," he said. "Maggie Dunlop has disappeared. I went myself in a squad car round to Nelson Mandela House but the flat was empty, and the Tullyfeathers had gone as well. Someone in this station must be responsible. Perhaps it was meant as a joke?"

"Taking a joke a bit far when it meant faking those photographs," pointed out Hamish, who was beginning to enjoy himself.

"Dear me, yes. There will be a full investigation. Have you yourself any idea who...? What about that policewoman, Mary Graham, who had some sort of spite against you?"

"Oh, I shouldn't think it was her," said Hamish blithely. "This has upset me a lot, sir. Do you mind if I go home?"

"By all means. You are taking this remarkably well, Hamish. If there is anything I can do for you, anything at all..."

Willie, thought Hamish, but not yet.

He said goodbye and ambled down the stairs and into the detectives' room and looked around. There was no sign of Blair. He was not surprised. He went out and had a meal and then returned to the detectives' room. This time, Blair was sitting at his desk.

"Oh, aye, Hamish," he said with false heartiness. "Glad ye got that wee problem sorted out."

Hamish pulled up a chair close to Blair and leaned forward. "Don't ever do that again," he whispered, "and unless you get me the central heating for my police station, I'll track down that brass nail you coerced into lying and I'll have *you* out of a job."

"I don't know whit you're talking about," muttered Blair.

"Do I get the central heating or not?"

"Aye, of course, Hamish. I promised, didn't I? Mind you, Daviot's cutting down on regional expenses and—"

"You've got a week," said Hamish and rose and left.

Blair watched him go and then lumbered to his feet. He caught Mr. Daviot just as the superintendent was leaving.

"I saw Macbeth," said Blair. "He's in a fair taking over the way he's been treated."

"Oh, dear," said Mr. Daviot. "He seemed so good about it all. Of course I did tell him if there was anything we could do for him to let us know."

"As tae that, I meant to tell you, sir, that he's been wanting the central heating for that bit o' a polis station in Lochdubh."

"Then arrange it! Arrange it right away!"

"Yes, sir. Right away, sir. How's the lady wife, sir?"

"Tolerably well, thank you. She was delighted with the flowers you sent her."

"Only too happy tae please, sir, you know that."

Blair followed the superintendent down the stairs, oiling and complimenting. Superintendent Daviot saw nothing wrong with this. In fact, he enjoyed it immensely.

Blair finally got back to his desk. What had come over him to try that trick on Hamish? He had been so pleased with the job he'd done on those photographs. Now he'd had to pay Maggie and the Tullyfeathers to run for it—pay them a lot. It must have been the drink. He would never drink again. Well, maybe just the one to steady his nerves. He slid open the bottom drawer of his desk and eased the bottle out.

Hamish drove slowly and carefully back to Lochdubh. It was so cold that even the salty slush on the roads was beginning to freeze hard.

A small cold moon was shining down on the snow-covered moors. He braked hard as a stag skittered across the road in front of him. He drove on through the moon landscape until he topped the rise of the road which led down to Lochdubh. Bright stars were burning above and shining in the still waters of the loch below. Home, he thought, home and comfort. A glass of whisky, light the fire, relax.

But when he pulled up at the police station it was to see the kitchen door and front door standing open and piles of furniture in the small drive at the side. From the inside came the busy sound of vacuuming.

He edged his way around the furniture and walked in.

Willie was through in the living-room. He was pushing the vacuum around the carpet and whistling cheerfully.

"Willie!" roared Hamish, bending down and whipping the vacuum cord so that the plug shot out of the wall.

Willie turned slowly and stared at Hamish in ludicrous dismay. "It's yerself."

"What the hell are you doing to my home?" demanded Hamish.

"I thought I waud give it a wee bittie o' a spring-clean," said Willie miserably.

"Get this straight," said Hamish. "You occupy one bedroom. The rest is mine—my furniture, my books, my carpet, my kitchen...mine, mine, mine. Put everything back the way it was, close the doors, heat the place up. You've got one hour to do it. And don't ever let me see you do any housekeeping here again."

Hamish turned and strode out. Willie blinked and looked slowly about at the ruin of his dream. Gone forever, oh lovely Regency-striped paper. Gone forever, synthetic dust-free log fire.

Hamish drove to Tommel Castle Hotel, parked and went in search of Priscilla.

She was in the hotel office, sitting in front of a computer. "Working late," commented Hamish.

"Yes, Mr. Johnson's got a bad cold." Mr. Johnson was the manager. "Sit down, Hamish. You don't look your usual relaxed self. What's up?"

He told her all about Blair's perfidy. "So," she said when he had finished, "that'll leave a gap in the ranks."

"How come?"

"Well, Blair'll be out on his ear."

"No, he won't. I didn't tell Daviot I knew it was Blair."

"Why not?"

"I told Blair to get the central heating put in instead."

"Hamish Macbeth, no detective should be allowed to stay in the force after pulling a trick like that. Forget about the central heating. Get on to the phone now and tell Daviot you know it was Blair."

"No point in that," said Hamish uneasily. "He'll have destroyed any evidence in his dark-room, and that precious pair he got to bear false witness will be long gone."

"They can be found," snapped Priscilla. "You know that."

Hamish looked at her in irritation. "Look, Blair's had it in for me for a long time. I can cope. He's not bent when it comes to the general public. In fact, he's quite a good policeman in his plodding way."

"When he's not coercing one ex-prostitute and one ex-burglar to lie for him to get you out of a job!"

"Priscilla, let it go. It's my business, not yours."

She eyed him coldly. "You're a born moocher. When it comes to getting something for nothing, then you'd turn a blind eye to murder."

"That iss going too far!"

They both stared at each other in dislike. Hamish seized his cap, which he had placed on her desk when he arrived, noticing that the brim was cracked, for it was his second-best one, his good one having been lost in the river when he rescued the boy. "I haff nothing mair tae say tae ye," said Hamish, stalking out and spoiling the effect by knocking into an umbrella-stand at the door and sending the contents flying. He picked up the assortment of walking-sticks and umbrellas and shoved them back into the uprighted stand.

Outside, he got into the car. He did not want to go straight back to the police station. He decided to call on Dr. Brodie and his wife, Angela.

The doctor welcomed him, saying Angela was off at Stirling University on some course to do with her Open University degree. Hamish told him the tale of Blair and the doctor laughed appreciatively. "So you'll be getting the central heating at last. How's that wee moron of yours getting on?"

Correctly identifying the moron as Willie, Hamish told him of the spring cleaning of the police station. "That's bad," said Dr. Brodie, shaking his head. He handed Hamish a glass of whisky and then shovelled two dogs off the sofa so that Hamish could find a place to sit down. "Remember when Angela had that spell of frantic cleaning? Man, it was terrible. Each house should have a little of its own family dirt. Gives the place character. I see you've still got your beatniks up at the back of the manse."

"They don't call them beatniks any more," said Hamish gloomily, still thinking of Priscilla's angry face. "They call themselves the travellers or new travellers and try to claim the same rights as the gypsies. That pair has me fair puzzled. You see, normally these travellers like to go around in convoys, making some landowner's life hell. Landowner screams for the police, complains his land is being turned into a sewer, that the travellers' children aren't going to school and that drugs are traded openly. If he has enough power, then the police come in to move them on. Press arrive in droves. Next day letters in the papers from Church of England vicars and so on, complaining about harassing these poor innocent people, and the landowner is nothing but a bloated capitalist. A few people complain that the travellers are allowed to run around without road taxes and on bald wheels and all the other crimes for which John Smith is regularly stopped by the police and hauled over the coals, and then by the following day it's all forgotten until the travellers cause the next batch of trouble and then it all starts up again. But this pair have admittedly an old bus, but the tax is paid and he's got a clean license and the tyres are good. What are they after?"

"Maybe not after anything," said Dr. Brodie, throwing another lump of peat on the ash-choked fire. "Maybe genuine drifters."

"Then there was Priscilla's scarf. She said he'd taken it. Mrs. Wellington says she's probably dropped it behind the counter, and sure enough, there it is."

"Priscilla doesn't make mistakes," said Dr. Brodie.

"No, she's barely human, and that's a fact," complained Hamish.

Dr. Brodie gave him a quizzical look, waiting for more, but instead Hamish said, "If only I could get some lassie to fancy Willie and take him off my hands."

"There's another way you could go about it," said the doctor slyly.

"Aye, what's that?"

"Get married yourself."

"There's nobody I fancy."

"Except Priscilla. Forget Priscilla. Do you know Priscilla? I've known her since she was a wee lassie and I don't really know her. Very self-contained. She'll eventually marry the right bloke, some land-owner, and we'll never know whether it was love or whether she was doing the right thing to please her parents. What about that new luscious lovely at the restaurant?"

"Lucia? Oh, everyone's after her, including Willie, and Willie hasn't a hope in hell. I gather his idea of courtship is telling her how to scrub the steps and clean the cooker."

"There's Maisie Gowan."

"Maisie Gowan's eighteen years old!"

"What's up wi' that? She fancies you. Then there's that Doris Ward from the hotel."

"No, not her," said Hamish. "I don't want anyone. I want my old life back. I want rid of Willie. Man, this power is the terrible thing. When I had no one to boss but myself, I was that easygoing. Now I breathe down Willie's neck and snap if he doesn't haff the paperwork chust the way it should be. Ach, the man's a fair scunner, but I make things worse."

"Never mind. Have another whisky," said the doctor. "It's this bitter weather. Very claustrophobic. The good weather'll be along soon and everything will be more open and relaxed."

"Is there anything on the telly?" asked Hamish, looking longingly at the set in the corner. "Willie had one but he got rid of it because he says he doesn't believe in it, chust as if it wass a type of religion."

"Wait and I'll look up the paper and see what's on," said the doctor, judging by the hissing sibilancy of Hamish's Highland accent that he was really upset. "Here we are, BBC 1: 'Whither England? Mary Pipps of the former Communist Party discusses plans for a European future.' Dear me. BBC 2: 'The rape of the Brazilian rain forests.' Not again. You know what's caused the demise of the Brazilian rain forests, Hamish? Camera crews trudging all over the place. Grampian: 'The Reverend Mackintosh of Strathbane Free Presbyterian Church gives his view on the spread of AIDS in Africa.' Nothing left but Channel 4, let me see...ah, 'Highlights of the Gulf War,' a repeat of last year's showing. Well, Hamish?"

"None of that. Can I take a look through your paperbacks and borrow a hot-water bottle? Willie threw my hot-water bottle out. He said the rubber was perished."

"You sound like a man with a nagging wife. The books are over there; help yourself."

Hamish, after much deliberation, chose an American detective story of the tough-cop variety. He collected a hot-water bottle and then crunched his way out through the icy snow on the doctor's unswept garden path. Great stars still burnt overhead but were beginning to be covered with thin high trails of cloud. He sniffed the air. A change was coming. The air smelt damp, rain-damp, not the metallic smell of snow.

He drove slowly to the police station. The furniture was gone from outside. Inside, the stove was blazing merrily in the kitchen. Everything smelt damply of ammonia and disinfectant. He took a look around the rest of the place. Willie's bedroom door was tightly shut, a mute reproach to Hamish's lack of understanding about housekeeping. Hamish went back to the kitchen and sat in front of the fire and opened the detective story. In it, the detective had a blonde girlfriend whom he treated abominably, something which seemed to make her even more adoring. Long and careful questioning of suspects was out of the question. He simply slapped them around until he got the answers. It was as remote a way of life to Hamish as an Arthurian legend. He read happily and finally went to bed with much of his old good-natured frame of mind restored. Let Willie clean and scrub and write reports in convoluted English. If he just ignored the man and went about his own ways, then life would be tolerable. As for Priscilla...?

Pompous hard-faced bitch, he thought, clutching the comforting hot-water bottle to his stomach. Who needs her anyway?

The weather again went in for one of its abrupt changes and heralded in the morning light with a blast of wind which roared into the loch and departed at the other end with an eldritch screech. Following it came the rain, steady, drenching rain. Once more the River Anstey was in tumult and the bridge was being seriously damaged by the pressure of the roaring flood. The village council met to decide whether to opt for a completely new bridge by the side of the old one, a new one which could take two lanes of traffic. But the die-hards wanted the old bridge. It was picturesque and one of the much-photographed sights of the village.

Willie, sensing there was some sort of a truce, kept his housekeeping to a minimum, but when Hamish made no protest, he was soon happily back, polishing everything in sight.

But his happiness was dimmed by the fact that Lucia was walking out with Jimmy Gordon, the forestry worker. Jimmy was tall and fairly good-looking. Everyone in the village said they made a handsome couple.

Hamish had elected to do the outer reaches of the beat by car, leaving Willie to cover the village beat on foot. Somehow, wherever Jimmy walked with Lucia, Willie was never far behind.

"Would ye no' like tae come a bit o' a drive up in the hills wi' me?" Jimmy was asking Lucia. "We cannae get away from the polis."

Lucia shook her head. Mr. Ferrari said she was allowed to go for walks with Jimmy in the village and always where they could be seen. She glanced back at Willie and then said in her soft voice and very slowly, for she was always translating what she said in her mind from Italian to English, "What is your idea of marriage, Jeemy?"

He took her hand in his. "I want a wee wife to work and clean fur me, someone pretty tae come home tae in the evenings."

"Would you wish me to iron your shirts?"

"Aye, that would be grand. Look at this one. It's a' crumpled."

"Why don't you iron it yourself, Jeemy?"

He gave a great laugh and then flung an arm about her shoulders. "That's women's work."

Lucia gently disengaged herself.

Jimmy never knew what he had said wrong. But after that when he called at the kitchen door for Lucia, it was always old Mr. Ferrari who answered and who told him that Lucia was too busy to see him.

Chapter Four

They flee from me, that sometime did me seek.

—Sir Thomas Wyatt

The good weather did not come all at once. At first there was a lessening of the wind, then the rain decreased to a thin drizzle and soon the rain ceased altogether, letting fitful rays of watery sunlight through the clouds. The days grew perceptibly warmer until even Hamish Macbeth, who delighted in his new central heating, was forced to admit that the police station was becoming like a hothouse. And then one day all the clouds rolled back and pale-blue skies stretched above Lochdubh, and the River Anstey at long last settled back down into its familiar banks, leaving a path of torn trees and bleached grass on either side as a record of its recent fury.

But the coming of the idyllic weather made Hamish Macbeth realize that he was becoming oddly unpopular. Angela Brodie, the doctor's wife, went out of her way to avoid him, as did Mrs. Wellington. No more did Priscilla drop in on him for a chat. Even Nessie and Jessie Currie, the village spinster sisters, dived indoors and left their gardening tools scattered on the lawn when they saw him coming.

And for some reason, Hamish felt it all had something to do with Sean Gourlay. The bus was still there, looking to Hamish like a cancerous sore in the heart of the village. But he could not ask Sean to move on because of a feeling of evil, or rather a premonition of evil to come. He knew several of the villagers, the Misses Curries and Angela among them, had been visitors to the bus. Cheryl was occasionally to be seen about the village, much cleaned up and quiet, always on her own and talking to no one. Hamish was sure Sean had started some campaign to turn the villagers against him.

And then there was the strange behaviour of Mr. Wellington, the minister. Like most churches these days, Mr. Wellington's was sparsely attended, although the organizations connected with the church were as busy as ever. Most women in the village belonged to the Mothers' Union, of which Mrs. Wellington was the chairwoman. The Boy Scouts and Girl Guides were both well attended. But gradually the church began to fill up on Sundays and Hamish was surprised to see members of the Free Presbyterian Church, members from the Free Church of Scotland, and from the Uni-

tarians all neglecting their own kirks to go and hear
Mr. Wellington preach. What could be the reason?
Hamish decided to find out. He told Willie to man the
phone in the police office and went along to the church
himself, meeting the fisherman, Archie Maclean, and
his wife on the way.

"I've never known you to go to the kirk before," said
Hamish.

"Aye, but this is different," said Archie. "Mr. Wellington preaches a rare sermon. We've heard naethin'
like it since the auld days."

Hamish was intrigued. On his rare visits to church,
he had tried to keep awake as Mr. Wellington's gentle
scholarly voice wrestled with one of the more esoteric
points of the Bible. Hamish often thought it sounded as
if the minister were reasoning with himself.

He slid into a pew at the back.

The hymns were of the variety now frowned upon
by liberal churchmen of all denominations as being too
militant: "Stand Up, Stand Up for Jesus, Ye Soldiers of
the Cross," and "Onward, Christian Soldiers."

Then the minister climbed up into the high pulpit
and looked down at a sheaf of yellowing notes. Hamish
was surprised. Before, the minister's sermons had been
extempore, or rather so well rehearsed that he spoke
without notes.

Then he suddenly looked down at his flock and
said in a harsh voice Hamish had never heard him use

before, "There are many of you here who will all burn in hell!"

There was a pleasurable indrawing of breath. Mrs. Maclean edged a peppermint into her mouth. For some reason it was considered all right to eat peppermints in church, although chocolates would be considered downright sinful.

"Yes," went on the minister, "there are many of you who are liars and fornicators, and your lot will be to be cast into the pit where your flesh will fry, yea, and your crackling skin will be pricked with pitchforks by demons."

The sermon ranted on for one hour and forty minutes. Hamish sat stunned. It was only when the minister summed up by asking them all to pray to God to protect them from the evil that was Napoleon Bonaparte that a glimmer of understanding began to dawn in his hazel eyes.

Curious and beginning to be half-worried, half-amused, he also went to the evening service. He was late and had to stand at the back, for the church was full to overflowing.

He was among the last to leave. He shook Mr. Wellington's hand and said quietly, "Can I drop up to the manse and have a word with you?"

"Yes, Hamish," said the minister absent-mindedly. "I shall be there to hear your troubles."

"It's your troubles I'm thinking about," said Hamish,

but the minister was already shaking hands with a couple behind him and receiving their plaudits.

Hamish went up to the manse later, glad to find the minister on his own.

"What can I do for you?" asked Mr. Wellington.

"What's come over you?" asked Hamish. "You never were a one for all that fire and brimstone."

"It brings people to church and instills a fear of God in them which is what I am here for," said the minister primly.

"But it's not like you," expostulated Hamish. "You know what I think? I think that one day you couldn't think of a sermon and so you found some old ones and used one of them instead. Instant success! So you went on doing it. You're a walking horror movie. You'll have the children terrified to go to sleep at night. You don't even listen to what you're saying, which is why you left in the bit about Napoleon."

The minister flushed angrily and glared at the wall.

"Come on, what's been happening?" asked Hamish gently.

Mr. Wellington clasped his hands and swung to face Hamish. "I've lost my faith," he said. "No words of mine have any meaning any more. In despair, yes, I used old sermons I found in a box in the attic. It's what they want. It brings them to the kirk."

"Aye, so would a strip-tease. Surely you've lost your faith afore? It happens from time to time."

"No, never."

Hamish leaned back in his chair and clasped his hands behind his head. "Has this anything to do with Sean Gourlay?"

"He did question me," said the minister awkwardly. "People here do not question ministers, and maybe they should. We get complacent, arrogant. He showed me pictures of refugees stumbling along roads pitted with bomb craters, of thousands dying after floods and tornadoes, and he asked me seriously how I could believe in a God of love."

"But you can't defend the indefensible," said Hamish wearily. "Blind faith's the only answer, you know that. You must have had all thae arguments dinned in your ears when you were a student."

"I am out of the world up here, Hamish. As Sean rightly pointed out, I have an easy life while millions are starving and suffering under the lash of the God I worship."

"There are millions who would suffer a damn sight more if they didnae have something tae believe in," said Hamish angrily. "How dae ye think they would feel if they were told that this is it, this is all there is, and after the grave, there is nothing?"

"My wife feels the same as I do," he said heavily. "It has affected her badly. She is a shadow of her former self."

Spiritually but not physically, thought Hamish, who

had seen the large tweedy bulk of Mrs. Wellington in church that evening. "Don't make any rash decisions," said Hamish. "Give it a few months. Talk to some other members of the clergy. Father Peter along at the Roman Catholic church seems a good man, and a clever one, too. Have a word with him."

The minister smiled wryly. "I do not know what my flock would think if they saw me consulting a Roman Catholic."

"We're all ecumenical these days," pointed out Hamish. "Anyway, no one need know. Run along and see him. It's all the one God."

When Hamish left, he strolled along the waterfront wondering if he himself believed anything he had said, wondering if there really was anything far beyond the first stars which were beginning to glitter in a pale-green sky.

With a sigh he went into the police station, to be met with a delicious smell. "You're late for dinner," said Willie, sliding a plate of beef casserole, which smelt of rich wine sauce, onto the table.

"Where did this come from?" asked Hamish.

"Mr. Ferrari," said Willie, deftly opening a bottle of Italian wine.

He's been cleaning the restaurant stove again, thought Hamish, but was too grateful for the delicious meal to say so.

After dinner, the phone rang. It was Jimmy Anderson

from Strathbane. "I took pity on ye, Hamish," said the detective, "and contacted the Yard. Sean Gourlay's got a record."

"Tell me about it," said Hamish eagerly.

"Nothing great, mind you, petty larceny, possession of cannabis, disturbance of the peace. Nothing for the last three years. Was in Hong Kong, where he got his first driving license. Let it lapse and took the test in Glasgow."

"Well, send me up a report," said Hamish. "It might do to get him off the manse field and out of this village."

Willie came into the police office. "The doctor's here tae see you," he said.

Hamish rang off and turned to face an agitated Dr. Brodie. "I was making an inventory of the drugs cabinet, Hamish, and there's four packets of morphine missing."

"I'd better come down and have a look at the cabinet. I cannae remember. Is it easy tae get into?" asked Hamish.

"No, it's padlocked and it's got a metal grille over it."

"And nothing's been broken?"

"Not that I can see."

Hamish dialed Strathbane and reported the theft, asking for a forensic team to be sent up in the morning. "And while you're at it," he said, "get me a search warrant for Sean Gourlay's bus."

"What, the traveller?" exclaimed the doctor. "But he hasn't been near the surgery."

"Well, we'll see," said Hamish. "Come on, Willie. Let's go and have a look." They followed the doctor to his home.

Angela, the doctor's wife, gave Hamish a nervous look. "Isn't it terrible?" she gasped.

"We'll see if we can find any clues," said Hamish. Dr. Brodie collected the keys to the surgery, which was along the road from his home.

Hamish examined the locks of the surgery carefully and then, inside, inspected the cabinet. "When do you think the packets of morphine were taken?" he asked.

"That's the devil of it," said Dr. Brodie. "I haven't really checked anything for six months. This is all I need."

"Well, we'd best lock everything up again and let no one near it until after the forensic team's arrived," said Hamish.

Hamish fully expected Detective Chief Inspector Blair to arrive on the following morning, but it was an Inspector Turnbull, a dour Aberdonian who arrived with Detective Jimmy Anderson and three uniformed policemen as well as the forensic team. He had a search warrant for Sean's bus and listened carefully as Hamish described Sean's criminal record.

Sean and Cheryl were brought down to the police station, where they were both searched, and then Sean was asked to take them to the bus.

Sean opened the door for them and then examined

the search warrant again carefully. "If you and your lady will just step outside," said Inspector Turnbull, "we'll be as quick as we can."

The day was fine and mild. Sean and Cheryl sat side by side on a large packing case on the grass. Hamish noticed that they did not speak to each other.

He found himself praying to the God he was not quite sure he believed in for drugs to be found. He felt Sean was an evil influence on the village and wanted him out of it.

At long last, Turnbull emerged. "Nothing," he said to Hamish.

"Great stinking pigs," muttered Cheryl, but Sean put a hand on her arm and remarked pleasantly, "You really must stop harassing us, Inspector, just because we don't fit into any conventional pattern."

"Oh, I wouldnae say that," said Turnbull. "There's a lot o' you long-haired layabouts crawling about Scotland."

"My hair is not long, and if you don't watch your mouth, Inspector, I shall sue you for harassment. You've found nothing, so shove off."

Hamish suddenly said, "Better check under the bus, Inspector, just in case."

He had the satisfaction of seeing a look of alarm on Cheryl's face.

Sean lit a cigarette and eyed Hamish through the smoke. "Determined to find me guilty, eh? I think it's time I phoned the press."

He loped off in the direction of the manse. Hamish watched while the Calor gas tank outside the bus was unhitched, as were the cables from the bus to the manse, Sean obviously leeching electricity supplies from the minister. The keys, as Cheryl informed them, were in the blank, blank, blanking ignition. The bus roared into life and moved forward.

To Hamish's delight, there were loose sods of earth under the bus which, when lifted, revealed a hole about three feet square, recently dug. But it turned out to be full of rubbish—Coke cans, bottles and scraps of paper.

Whatever had been hidden there, and Hamish was sure something had been hidden there, had gone. But who could have alerted Sean? Willie was a gossip, but Willie had been close to him, Hamish, since the doctor had first reported the theft.

Cheryl put up an arm to brush her hair out of her eyes. Her loose sleeve rolled back. Hamish saw ugly bruises on her thin arm.

But there was nothing he could do about that unless Cheryl showed any signs of wanting to report Sean for beating her up, and from the way she had suddenly started to scream obscenities at the police, it was highly doubtful if she ever would. But what did Mrs. Wellington think when she heard the girl running off at the mouth like that? Possibly she hadn't heard her. Possibly Cheryl reserved her swear-words for the police.

Next day the *Strathbane and Highland Gazette*

carried a photograph of Sean and Cheryl on the front page. Sean was looking like a film star and Cheryl was attired in a pretty-pretty flowered cotton dress, with her hair done in two pigtails. The article quoted Sean as saying that they were a couple who only wanted to be left alone to enjoy the beautiful Highlands of Scotland but that they were being persecuted by the police. Inspector Turnbull was correctly quoted, describing Sean as a long-haired layabout. The article finished by saying that the couple were living in a converted bus on manse land with the full approval of the minister and his wife.

So that was that, apart from a stern warning from Strathbane not to go near the couple again unless evidence was concrete.

Sean and Cheryl had purchased from somewhere a small motor scooter, and one day, they roared off on it. But their bus still stood up on the manse field. Hamish, however, was glad to see them go, and hoped they would stay away for a few days at least.

But while they were gone, Hamish received an agitated caller, the treasurer of the Mothers' Union, Mrs. Battersby. She was a thin, pale woman in her mid-forties with thick glasses, wispy hair and dressed in a wool two-piece she had knitted herself out of one of Patel's "special offers," a sulphurous-yellow yarn.

"There's one hundred pounds missing from the kitty," she said.

Hamish's thoughts immediately flew to Sean. "When do you think it was taken?" he asked.

"Let me see, I counted it on Sunday, for Mrs. Anderson had given me ten pounds. We have been collecting for Famine Relief. Then this morning, Mrs. Gunn gave me five pounds and I opened up the box to add that money to it and thought I'd better just count it all over again and log it in the book and I immediately saw that one hundred pounds had gone!"

Hamish's heart sank. Sean and Cheryl had left last Saturday. They couldn't have taken it.

"How much was there altogether?" he asked.

"One hundred and forty-five pounds and twenty-three pee."

"It's a wonder the lot wasn't taken."

"Ah, you see, the hundred was in notes and the remainder is just in small change."

"I'd better come along and hae a look," said Hamish. "Willie, you come as well."

Willie, who had come through from the kitchen, began to remove his apron. "Aye, thon's the grand lad you have there," said Mrs. Battersby despite her distress at the theft. "Always cleaning."

Hamish, in order to keep relations with Willie as easy as possible, had allowed the policeman to continue housekeeping. It seemed to be Willie's only interest in life. A new cleaner on the market was judged by Willie with all the care of a connoisseur sampling a rare wine. It was a pity, thought Hamish, that he had under him a policeman who showed so little interest in policing.

They walked together towards the church hall. "So the funds are kept here," said Hamish. "I would have thought you would have kept them at home."

"The reason I did not," said Mrs. Battersby, "is because of the great responsibility of it all. If any went missing in my home, then I would get the blame."

"There's a lot o' wickedness around," said Willie. "The minister was saying only last Sunday that it creepeth like the serpent and stingeth like the adder."

"That's booze, not burglary," snapped Hamish, distressed at this evidence that the minister was still reading out ancient hell-fire sermons.

There was a small group of women outside the church hall, headed by Mrs. Wellington, her face white with distress.

"Who could have done such a thing?" she cried when she saw them.

"Chust let me see where the money was kept," said Hamish.

Mrs. Wellington produced a massive key and unlocked the church hall. She led the way into the kitchen and opened a cupboard under the sink. There, among the cleaners and dusters, was a tin box with a small padlock. The padlock had been broken.

"Now that's verra interesting," said Willie.

"What is?" demanded Hamish.

"Judge's Lemon Shine," said Willie, holding up a bottle. "That'll no' get ye verra far with the cleaning, ladies. It's no good with the grease."

"Get out of the way," muttered Hamish, exasperated. He took a large handkerchief out of his pocket and gently lifted the box up onto the kitchen counter. "Any sign of a break-in?" he asked. "Any broken windows?"

"Nothing at all," said Mrs. Battersby.

"So who's got the key to the hall?"

There was a shamefaced silence and then one woman said, "It's kept under the doormat outside. Anyone could have got it."

"There's not much I can do, ladies," said Hamish, "short of fingerprinting the whole village, and even then I doubt if I'd find the prints of the thief on the box. There's probably only your fingerprints on it, Mrs. Battersby."

A small, angry-looking woman, Mrs. Gunn, said, "I notice ye got a new microwave the last week, Mrs. Battersby."

"What are you saying?" squeaked Mrs. Battersby. "Me, that's worked so hard for Famine Relief, to take that money!"

"We won't get to the bottom of this if you're all going to maliciously accuse each other," said Hamish sharply. "Now the money was all right on Sunday. This is Wednesday. Who's been in the hall since then?"

"The Guides use it on Monday evening," volunteered Mrs. Wellington, "and the Boy Scouts on Tuesday evening."

"Bessie Dunbar's the Guide captain," said Mrs. Gunn, "and herself came back from Inverness on Monday wi' a new coat."

"Enough!" roared Hamish, upset by the malice, upset by the fact that the usually indomitable Mrs. Wellington had begun to cry. "I need a list of all the members of the Mothers' Union. Willie, you start taking statements from those here. Mrs. Wellington, go home and get a cup of tea or something and I'll call on you later."

By the end of the day, Hamish thought wearily that some of the murder cases he had previously worked on had been clean and innocent compared to the spite and malice roused by the theft of the Mothers' Union funds. Everyone seemed eager to accuse everyone else. Any woman who had a new purchase of any kind was evidently suspect. He doggedly went round the village taking statement after statement, ending up at the manse with Mrs. Wellington.

"This iss a bad business," mourned Hamish. "I thought ye were all such friends, and now one's accusing the other." He turned on the minister, who was slumped in an armchair by the fire. "This village is in

sore need of a lecture on common decency. I suggest
you start thinking of them and less about yourself and
give them a sermon about the wickedness of bearing
false witness against their neighbour. I neffer thought
to see the day in Lochdubh. If I believed in the devil,
then I'd say he'd come among you!"

"Maybe he has," said Mrs. Wellington, scrubbing at
her red eyes with a damp handkerchief.

"Havers," snorted Hamish. "Where are the funds now?"

"Nobody trusts poor Mrs. Battersby or anyone else,"
said Mrs. Wellington. "So I took what's left to the bank
and lodged it with the manager."

Hamish asked a string of questions, trying to find
out if anyone from outside had been seen in the village,
but there was no one. There were guests up at Tommel Castle Hotel who had arrived on Sunday, but none
as yet had come down to the village, the guests having
been out on the river on the colonel's estate, fishing.

At last he made his way from the manse and then
stopped in surprise outside the trim cottage owned by
Jessie and Nessie Currie. A "For Sale" sign was placed
by the garden gate.

Now the sisters, although often a pain in the neck to
Hamish with their frequent remarks that he was a lazy
lout, *were* Lochdubh, as much a part of the scenery as
the twin mountains which rose above the village, and
the sea loch in front of it.

He had interviewed them earlier, for both, although

spinsters, were members of the Mothers' Union. He walked up to the door and knocked.

A lace curtain twitched beside the window and then there was a long silence. He knocked again. Jessie answered the door. "Oh, it's yourself," she said. "It's yourself." Jessie often repeated herself, like the brave thrush, as if she never could recapture the first fine careless rapture of her original sentences.

"You didnae tell me you were thinking of moving," said Hamish.

"Why should we? Why should we?" demanded Jessie and then slammed the door in his face.

Hamish walked sadly away.

He was hailed by Dr. Brodie. "I'm going to the pub for a dram," said the doctor. "Care to join me?"

"Aye, I'd be glad to get the taste of this day out of my mouth."

"I heard what happened," said Dr. Brodie. "First the morphine and then this theft of money and the only people who might have taken the stuff are Sean and Cheryl, but the drugs weren't found on them and they were definitely out of the village when the money was stolen."

"Everything's gone bad and wrong," mourned Hamish. "You should have heard these women, all hinting that one or the other one of them had stolen the funds. Jessie and Nessie Currie have put their house up for sale."

"What?" The doctor stopped short in amazement. "Why? What's happened?"

"I don't know. Jessie answered the door but she wouldn't talk to me. Everyone in this village has changed for the worse since Sean arrived."

They walked into the bar. Dr. Brodie bought two double whiskies and they sat down at a small table in the corner. The juke-box was belting out a country-and-western number which eventually twanged to a halt, leaving a blessed silence.

"Angela's gone funny again," said the doctor.

"But she's been doing so well, studying for her degree," said Hamish, "and she's been so happy."

"She's gone edgy of late and she keeps asking me for money for clothes. Angela! I could have sworn Angela didn't know what was on her back half the time. Do you know, Hamish, she came back from Inverness last week with a dress that cost three hundred pounds! Three hundred! I didn't know there was a shop in Inverness that sold anything as expensive as that."

"Oh, Inverness is a boom town," said Hamish. "There's all sorts of shops now. Maybe we're behind the times. Maybe three hundred pounds is not an odd price for a frock."

"Maybe not in Bond Street, but it's a hell of a price to pay for something to wear around the hills and glens."

"Is it a verra grand frock?"

"I'm no judge. It's just black, and the only thing about it is that it's got a Christian Dior label."

"Are you worried she's fallen in love with someone else?" asked Hamish.

"There can't be anyone else. If you're thinking of Sean Gourlay, forget it. Oh, she took the odd cake and things over to the bus, but then she's like that. Always ready to welcome any newcomer to the village. But after the initial visits, she lost interest. There's something secret and nervy about her. I got out my torch and examined her eyeballs in case she had been taking the drugs for herself."

"Well, that's enough to put any woman off her husband, for a start," said Hamish.

"Aye, but I had to *know*. It's not drugs. She's plain miserable. One minute she's all over me, and the next, she's telling me to get lost."

"Sean Gourlay . . ." began Hamish.

"Forget it," sighed Dr. Brodie. "Admit it, you've had a bee in your bonnet about that one since he came here."

"But everything's gone wrong since he came here," protested Hamish. "Everything's wrong, everything's polluted. Mr. Wellington's lost his faith and is ranting rubbish from the pulpit which was written in the last century, and he doesn't believe a word of it. Mrs. Wellington's a wreck, Jessie and Nessie are selling up, and the women at the Mothers' Union are that spiteful, you wouldnae believe it. There's something at the back of it all, and I mean to find out!"

*   *   *

The next morning, Sean and Cheryl returned. The next afternoon, they had a public row on the waterfront. Cheryl called Sean every name under the sun. She was astride the scooter and had a rucksack on her back. The fluency of her obscenities amazed the villagers, the mothers clamping their hands over their children's ears but continuing to listen themselves.

Shorn of obscenities, Cheryl's complaint was that she was sick of the village and sick of Sean and she was leaving and she would not be back.

Sean shrugged and smiled lazily and then loped off with long strides, up towards the manse. Cheryl drove off on the scooter, put-putting her way out of Lochdubh, over the newly repaired hump-backed bridge, up the long road which led past Tommel Castle Hotel and out of sight.

One down, thought Hamish Macbeth savagely, and one to go.

Chapter Five

*There's a great deal to be said
For being dead.*

—E. C. Bentley

After a week of squally, sleety rain, the weather
became balmy again and the waters of the loch still.
Sea-gulls cruised lazily overhead, swooping occasionally to admire their reflections and then soaring
effortlessly up again. On the surface, Lochdubh looked
much the same as ever. Smells of strong tea and tar and
peat-smoke. Sounds of radio, clattering dishes, bleating
sheep, and chugging boats.

But underneath it all the theft of the Mothers' Union
funds spread like a cancer. Hamish, after wondering
how long Priscilla meant to ignore him, eventually
caved in and took the single-track road up out of the
village to the hotel.

He felt a slight pang when he saw her busy in the

gift shop, her smooth blonde hair lit by a shaft of sun-light. She was selling expensive souvenirs to a group of men who, Hamish noticed with irritation, were taking a long time about their purchases.

At last the shop was empty. Priscilla gave Hamish a guarded look and said, "Coffee?"

"That would be grand. Haven't seen you around for a bit."

"I've been here, you know," said Priscilla with an edge on her voice. "I gather you and Doris had a pleasant dinner last week."

"*She* invited me," said Hamish defensively, for he felt guilty at having accepted the invitation, knowing he had only done it in the hope that Doris would tell Priscilla, which she evidently had.

Priscilla handed him a mug of coffee. "Well, let's hope our new receptionist doesn't fall for you as well."

"New receptionist? What's happened to Doris?"

"Dear me. Didn't she tell you? She left. She's got a job in a hotel in Perth."

Hamish felt nothing but relief. Doris had all but proposed to him and it had been an agonizing and embarrassing evening.

"Well, what's been going on?" asked Priscilla. "I heard about the money disappearing from the Mothers' Union."

"Oh, it's the bad business." Hamish pulled a chair up to the counter and sat down. "All the women are at each other's throats, the one accusing the other. Dr. Brodie's had four packets of morphine stolen and the only suspect was Sean, but he was searched and we couldn't find anything. His girlfriend's gone off but the bastard's still there, like some canker in the middle of the village."

"It's those demonic good looks of his, Hamish. He's just a small-time crook, not the devil. I know he took that scarf and then slipped it back somehow."

"He's doing a rare job, nonetheless. He's managed to talk Mr. Wellington out of his faith and Mr. Wellington has been using some old sermons he found and it's all hell-fire and damnation and they love it. Archie Maclean told me he gave up seeing a video of *The Werewolf Women of Planet Xerxes* because, to quote him, 'the kirk was better fun.' You should hear those sermons. A real medieval hell, wi' devils and pitchforks and weeping and wailing and gnashing of teeth. I tried to get him to talk to the priest, I tried to get him to preach kindness and love thy neighbour, but the man's sunk in gloom. Mrs. Wellington looks a wreck. Nessie and Jessie Currie are selling up and leaving, and what that's got to do with Sean I don't know, but I feel it has. Angela Brodie's gone on the twitch again and this time is spending a fortune on clothes."

"It sounds awful. How's Willie?"

"I don't know whether the lad's smitten with Lucia Livia, or whether it's the dirty stoves at the restaurant he's after. He lives to clean. Look at that!" Hamish held up one glittering black boot for her inspection. "Even the insoles are polished. Look at my shirts! Starched, every one of them. I've got such knife-edged creases in my trousers, it's a wonder I don't cut myself."

"Some people would think you were lucky," pointed out Priscilla, "living as you do with a combination of housekeeper and valet."

"No, it iss not! I sat down to my breakfast this morning and Willie screeches, 'A fly! A fly!' seizes a can of fly-killer and pumps it all over the kitchen and all over my food. If they ever take a blood sample from me, it'll be three parts insecticide and one part disinfectant. But I've got used to Willie. He's a kind-enough lad. He's jist stark-staring mad, that's all. No, I feel if I could sort Mr. Wellington out and get him to put some sense into the villagers, things would get better."

"I'll see what I can do," said Priscilla, unhitching her coat. "I'm just about to lock up for lunch-time anyway."

"You? What can you do?"

"He might just listen to me. It's worth a try."

"Well," said Hamish doubtfully, "do your best. Have you forgiven me?"

"For letting Blair get away with all sorts of mayhem? I still think that was bad of you, Hamish, but when have I ever been able to stay mad at you for long?"

"It's a long time since you've been to see me."

"I'm an old-fashioned girl. The gentlemen are supposed to call on me."

"Well, I'll call on you tonight and take you for dinner."

"Can't. The hotel's too busy. Sunday's free. Let's catch the hell-fire sermon and then go to the Napoli."

"Suits me. But see if you can do something with Mr. Wellington!"

Priscilla found the minister in his study. He was sitting in front of the fire, reading a book. "Oh, Miss Halburton-Smythe," he said in a dull voice, "what can I do for you?"

"I've been hearing about you from Hamish," said Priscilla.

The minister gave her a tortured look. "Ah, yes," he said with a weary sigh, "about my loss of faith."

"I am more concerned about you losing your marbles," said Priscilla incisively.

He turned his head away. "There is so much suffering in the world," he moaned, "and what can I do about it?"

"You could do something with your own parish. If everyone did some good about themselves, their family and their neighbours, the ripples might begin to spread outwards. I spoke to several of the village women before I came here. The place is riddled with spite. Instead of being sunk in self-absorption and self-pity, you might get off your bum and write a sermon to change the horrible spite and gossip of your parishioners. If you want your faith to come back to you, then you might start by acting as if you've got a heart and soul!"

Mr. Wellington's head jerked round and he glared at Priscilla. "There has often been talk that you might marry Hamish Macbeth," he said, "but now I think I know why the man is so reluctant to propose."

"Why, you old horror!" said Priscilla, quite unruffled.

He rose to his feet. "How dare you attack a minister of the Church!"

"Take a look at yourself in the mirror," said Priscilla. "Take a good hard look and then ask yourself if you are not looking at the most selfish man in the whole of Lochdubh. Forget about your lost faith. If it's such a terrible thing, don't you think you might try instilling some thoughts of faith, charity, and goodness into your flock? Why should they lose their faith, just because you've lost yours? I am going to hear your sermon on Sunday and I warn you, if you start reading out one of those old sermons, I will get to my feet and attack you in the middle of the church for being a fraud."

She marched out. Hamish was strolling along the waterfront. He came up to her. "How did you get on?" he asked.

"All right. I think a few gentle words were all that was needed."

*   *   *

The church was crowded as usual on Sunday. Priscilla and Hamish managed to find space in a pew at the back. "Look," said Priscilla, nudging Hamish. "There's your devil."

Sean Gourlay was standing beside a pillar at the side of the church but where he could command a good view of the pulpit. He was wearing a black shirt and black cords. His odd green eyes glittered strangely in the light.

"Come to see his handiwork," muttered Hamish.

There were hymns, a reading from the New Testament, and then the minister leaned forward over the pulpit.

A rustle of papers as peppermints were popped in mouths and then the congregation settled back to enjoy what Archie Maclean called "a guid blasting."

In a quiet, carrying voice, the minister began to talk of the theft of the funds. Sean crossed his arms and looked amused. The minister went on to say that this had caused malice and gossip in the village, turning one family against the other. His voice rose as he begged them to love their neighbour as themselves. His whole sermon seemed to be spoken directly to Sean. He spoke of the suffering in the world and reminded them that Jesus Christ had died on the cross for them. He said that the suffering in the village had been brought about by themselves. They had let one common theft poison their lives. "There is no place for evil in this village," he said. "Look into your hearts and pray for charity, pray for kindness, and pray to the Good Lord for forgiveness for your sins. Let us pray together."

Before he bent his head, Hamish noticed Sean walking quickly out of the church. It was silly, he told himself, to be so worried about one mere mortal, to be so superstitious, but somehow the minister's confrontation with Sean, and that was surely what it had been, reminded him of old tales he had heard when he was small in the long dark winter evenings of the black devil in man's form, walking into a Highland village one day and causing ruin and disaster.

A very subdued congregation shuffled out of the church. Mrs. Gunn shook hands with Mrs. Wellington and said they must think up a scheme to raise money to restore what had been taken and another woman patted Mrs. Battersby on the back and said she had been doing a grand job as treasurer and hoped she would go on doing so. Groups of people were standing around the graveyard outside, talking to each other.

Hamish shook Mr. Wellington's hand and said, "A grand sermon."

"Thank you," said the minister. Then he suddenly added, "Do not worry about Sean. I have a feeling he will be leaving us."

"And what was that supposed to mean?" asked Hamish over lunch. "Knowledge or the second sight?"

"I think, like you, he's decided Sean is the real reason

for all the misery. When you think of it, who else could have taken that money?"

"But he and Cheryl weren't even here!"

"They could have slipped back during the night. It's a simple matter to find the key and open up the village hall."

"Well, let's hope the minister's right. If Sean doesnae move on, I'll need to think of some way to get him moving! What did you say to Mr. Wellington to get him to see sense?"

"Just a few gentle and womanly words," said Priscilla.

Hamish looked at her with admiration. "Aye, it's a grand thing, a woman's touch," he said. "I must have been ower-blunt."

Mr. Wellington returned to the manse after evening service feeling comforted. By next week, he knew, his congregation would have dwindled to the usual small number, but instead of giving them what they wanted, he had given them what they sorely needed to hear. His wife had taken sleeping pills and gone to bed. He stared at the bulk of her sleeping form uneasily. She was taking a lot of sleeping pills these days.

He slept restlessly that night. At two in the morning, he got up to go to the bathroom. On his way, he peered out of a passage window which overlooked the manse field at the back. All the lights in the bus were blazing. He gave a little sigh. Supplying Sean with free electricity had been his wife's idea. She would have to tell Sean that they could do it no longer. He would speak to her in the morning, although it would be a difficult scene. Hamish had told her, he knew, about Sean's criminal record, but she had refused to take it seriously.

In the morning, on his way to the bathroom to shave, he once more looked out. It was a dark rainy morning and the lights were still blazing in the bus.

So when his wife tottered to the breakfast table, he snapped at her. "Get dressed and tell that young hooligan that you befriended that he is no longer to use our electricity. In fact, while you are at it, you can tell him to go. I am not letting him use the field any more."

"But you said you were in sympathy with these travellers," she protested.

"I've been a fool, but no longer. Go and give that young man his marching orders."

"I c-can't!"

His normally domineering wife was looking grey and crumpled.

Worry for her made him, like most husbands, angry instead of sympathetic.

"Don't be silly. If it makes you feel any better, tell him *I* am ordering him to go!"

Mrs. Wellington eventually, encased in a voluminous

waxed coat and rain-hat and Wellington boots, walked across the wet field to the bus.

She could hear the chatter from the television set inside. She knocked at the door and waited.

"Sean," she called tremulously, and knocked again.

No answer.

She longed to turn away, to forget about the whole thing, but her husband would want to know why. She knocked loudly this time and then, in sudden desperation, sudden longing to get the whole distasteful business over with, she rattled the handle of the door. It swung open.

"Look here, Sean..." she began, heaving her bulk inside.

She stopped short and her mouth opened in a soundless scream.

Sean Gourlay lay on his back on the floor. His face and head had been beaten to a pulp. Beside him on the floor lay a bloody sledge-hammer. On the table, on the small television screen, a woman chattered in that inane way early-morning presenters have, as if addressing an audience of children.

Mrs. Wellington backed to the door. Small thin sounds were issuing from her mouth. She felt faint but dared not faint and be found lying next to that...that *thing*.

She stumbled from the bus and weaved her way like a drunk across the field. She opened the back door of the manse and the sight of home and familiar objects loosened her vocal cords and she threw back her head and gave a great cry of "MURDER!" And once started, she could not stop.

Hamish Macbeth stood miserably in the manse field in the driving rain, with Willie beside him, while a forensic team went over the bus inch by inch. Detective Chief Inspector Blair was pacing up and down, wearing a deerstalker and an old Inverness cape, looking like someone in an amateur production of a Sherlock Holmes mystery. The only thing that was lightening Blair's gloom was the fact that it was a nice seedy murder: no toffs involved. Just a hippie with his head bashed in. He'd had a public row with his girlfriend, the girlfriend had killed him, it was only a matter of time before they picked her up. He loathed being back in Lochdubh, a locality he associated with success for Macbeth and failure for himself. There was no need for either Hamish or his sidekick to be hanging about in the rain, but Blair had kept them there to make them suffer; but as trickles of water began to run down inside his collar, he realized he was suffering as well and suggested they go back to the police station and discuss the matter there and let the forensic boys get on with their job.

"Well," began Blair, pausing for a moment in surprise as Willie put a coaster under his coffee-cup, "it's straightforward enough. This creep has a row wi' his lassie, lassie comes back and bang, crash, goodbye boyfriend."

"Was it murder wi' intentions?" asked Willie eagerly.

"If ye mean was her intention tae bash his head in, yes, you moron. Now the pathologist says death came frae thae blows from the sledge-hammer. Sledge-hammer belongs tae the manse. Whit dae ye think, Sergeant, that yer minister friend was at the sauce and slammed Sean Gourlay's head in?" Blair laughed heartily.

Hamish looked at him bleakly, his thoughts racing. He found he was hoping against hope that the murderer *was* Cheryl but for reasons he could not explain.

He began to give Blair a report on Sean's criminal background, reminding him of the theft of the morphine and the theft of the church money, although adding that both Sean and Cheryl had been away from the village when the money was taken.

The police station was pleasantly warm and Willie's coffee was good. "I'd best jist sit here by the phone," said Blair, "while you two go off and take statements. I want to know anyone who saw hide or hair of Cheryl Higgins or anyone who heard the sound of that scooter you were talking about during the night."

Hamish and Willie agreed to divide the village between them, Willie eagerly volunteering for the part which contained the Italian restaurant.

Despite the rain, little groups of people were standing about, peering anxiously up the hill towards the field at the back of the manse.

All day long, Hamish questioned and questioned, but no one had seen Sean after he had left the church and no one had seen Cheryl. Mrs. Wellington had given the police a photograph of Cheryl which she had taken shortly after the couple had first arrived. It was shown on the six o'clock news. By seven o'clock, Cheryl Higgins had walked into the police station at Strathbane, and Blair, hearing about it, had driven back to headquarters. By nine o'clock, Detective Jimmy Anderson phoned Hamish.

"Bad news," he said. "Cheryl Higgins has a cast-iron alibi."

"She can't have," exclaimed Hamish.

"Aye, but she has. She's been staying with a bunch of travellers in a field outside Strathbane and she's been playing the guitar in a group called Johnny Rankin and the Stotters—she being one o' the Stotters. The pathologist is checking the contents of Sean's stomach and he says the man was killed at a rough guess between ten in the evening and midnight. Cheryl was playing in Mullen's Roadhouse, you know, about two miles outside the town, from nine till one in the morning. Then she went on frae there to a party in Strathbane. Witnesses all along the way."

"But how reliable are the witnesses?" asked Hamish.

"Stotter means glue-sniffer, doesn't it? Is that how the group got its name?"

"Probably. Most o' them were away wi' the fairies when we tried to talk to them, but there was the audience, about forty decent, or fairly decent, witnesses. She could ha' slipped away from the party, for I don't know if any of that lot knew whether they were coming or going, but the point is the time of the murder and during that time she was performing in front of about forty people at the roadhouse."

"I'm surprised any band is allowed to play on the Sabbath in Strathbane," observed Hamish.

"It's outside the town, so nobody bothers."

"So where's this field she's living on?"

"On the Dalquhart Road out on the north side, about five miles out on the left. Belongs to Lord Dunkle, him what had the pop festivals back in the sixties. Still thinks he's a swinger, silly auld scunner that he is. She's living in a caravan with a couple called Wayne and Bunty Stoddart, old friends from Glasgow. She disnae look at all like the picture the minister's wife gave us, but it's her, all right. She's dyed her hair orange since the photo was taken. In Cheryl's humble opinion some bampot in Lochdubh upped wi' the sledge-hammer and give him fifty whacks, and good riddance to bad rubbish, she says."

"Did she suggest anyone?"

Anderson chuckled. "Aye, she did that."

"Who?"

"Sergeant Hamish Macbeth."

"Silly bitch."

"I'm telling you, that pleased Blair no end."

Hamish sighed. "So I suppose Blair'll be back tomorrow?"

"No, it'll be me and Harry MacNab. There's been a big robbery at the home of one of the super's friends, so Blair's jumped at that. He disnae care about the death o' a layabout. No press coverage in it for him."

"There's been a fair amount of press about today," said Hamish.

"Aye, but they willnae be there tomorrow. Nobody in that village of yours had a good word to say for Sean Gourlay. If they had all said something nice, then the press could have run a 'much-loved' type o' bit. Even the *Strathbane and Highland Gazette* have dropped it in case anyone remembers their touching piece about what a charming couple Sean and Cheryl were and being hounded by the nasty cops. They've found out from you and then Blair that Sean had a record."

"Any relative to claim the body?"

"Got a mother in London, respectable body by all accounts. Coming up tomorrow to see the procurator fiscal."

"I'm surprised the villagers turned out to be so down

on Sean. All I got when the couple first arrived was about the romance of the road and leave the poor souls alone."

"Believe me, the romance wore off, or maybe it's now that he's murdered and his past has come out, none of them want to confess to having had a liking for him. But you see what this means, Hamish?"

"I don't want to."

"I can see that. It means that mair than likely someone in Lochdubh did it."

Hamish groaned.

"Cheer up," said Anderson. "You might find an itinerant maniac, if you're lucky."

Hamish said goodbye and replaced the receiver. He pulled forward a sheet of paper. He would need to start with any villagers who had been on friendly terms with Sean. Top of the list were Mr. and Mrs. Wellington. Then Angela Brodie had been seen visiting the bus. Then came Nessie and Jessie Currie.

He sat back and looked dismally at the short list. He would need to detach his mind from the sore fact that these people were friends. So what had he?

Mr. Wellington: lost his faith after a discussion with Sean and started preaching old sermons.

Mrs. Wellington: nervous and agitated and not at all anything like her old, confident, bossy self.

Angela Brodie: acting strangely and buying expensive clothes.

Nessie and Jessie Currie: house up for sale, tetchy and miserable.

Well, forget about the murder, he would have to try to find out what Sean had done to these people. In the meantime, Willie could forgo his visits to the Napoli and keep questioning and asking in case anyone had seen a stranger that day.

Chapter Six

Suspicion all our lives shall be stuck full of eyes.

—Shakespeare

Despite Blair's lack of interest, the police were doing a thorough job. The forensic team came back to go over the bus again, inch by inch. The sledge-hammer was identified as belonging to the manse, but the bus was also full of items which Sean had borrowed from the Wellingtons. Mr. Wellington said the sledge-hammer was normally lodged in a shed at the end of his garden. He was not aware that Sean had borrowed it at any time. Hamish had had high hopes for that hidey-hole under the bus, but it turned out to be full of the same bits of rubbish as before. In a neutral voice, he told Harry MacNab and Jimmy Anderson of the women who had been friendly with Sean, relieved in a way that the detectives would be questioning them and not himself. Never before had he been so reluctant to investigate any case. Still, he could not resist asking them at the end of the day how they had got on.

"They're all white and shaken," said Anderson, "but that could be because of the shock. I mean, you've known all these women for some time now, Hamish, and you can hardly say that any one of them have shown criminal tendencies."

"Forget about the women; what about the minister?"

"Nice old boy, but odd, really odd. He said something about the hammer of God."

"He was probably quoting Chesterton," said Hamish, who had read the Father Brown stories.

"Whoever he was quoting, he seemed smug. He said he'd called on the Lord for help and the Lord had helped, that sort of thing. Was he always that daft?"

"Not that I ever guessed," said Hamish bleakly. "Did you tell the Currie sisters they would have to stay in the village until the investigation was over?"

"Why? I thought a trip to Inverness was a big adventure for that pair."

"Their house is up for sale."

"Not now, it isn't," said Anderson.

"So," said Hamish, "they were going to leave, Sean gets murdered, and they change their minds. Why?"

"Look, Hamish, I know you like these people, but you know more about them than anyone else, and you're going to have to ask some questions yourself."

Anderson was lying back in a chair in the police-station office, with his feet on the desk. Willie came in with a tray of coffee-cups, clucked in disapproval, put down the tray, picked up a newspaper and slid it under Anderson's feet.

"That's mair like a houseboy than a policeman," snorted MacNab when Willie had left the room, "but he makes a grand cup o' coffee."

"And there was nothing in the bus," pursued Hamish, "nothing at all."

"Not a clue," said Anderson. "No morphine, no hundred pounds, no letters."

"So what happens to the bus now?"

"Sean's mither phoned Mr. Wellington and said she was too distressed over her son's death to do anything about it at the moment, and so Mr. Wellington said the bus could stay where it was until she felt fit enough to come up and take it away, or any of his belongings. There'll be no trouble about it. Sean left a will, all right and proper, leaving everything to his mither."

"Odd," muttered Hamish. "Any more on his background?"

"Oh, aye, this'll set you back. He was in the Hong Kong police for about six months but got the push."

"Why?"

"Downright laziness. Should ha' been a man after your own heart, Hamish."

"But this lassie, Cheryl," pursued Hamish. "Is there any way o' shaking her alibi?"

"Not without about forty witnesses to say she was in Mullen's the whole evening."

"Damn, I'd like a word with her myself."

"That'd be stepping out of your parish. You cannae shake that alibi."

"Maybe. But I'd like to try all the same."

Anderson sighed and poured more coffee. "I think this is one case you're never going to solve, Hamish Macbeth. I feel it in ma bones."

And so it seemed, as the days dragged into weeks. The file on Sean Gourlay was not closed, but it might just as well have been. The bus remained up on the field at the back of the manse, a daily mute reminder to Hamish of failure. He had interviewed the Wellingtons, Angela Brodie and the Currie sisters several times, but there was no change in their statements. They had gone out of their way to welcome Sean and Cheryl to the village and then had ceased to see them. They had been nowhere near the bus on the night of the murder.

He decided in despair to risk the wrath of Strathbane and go over on his day off and see if he could talk to Cheryl.

He went to Mullen's first. A sprawling red brick building with a huge car-park, it was open twenty-four hours. A poster advertising various groups that neither Hamish nor possibly anyone else had ever heard of was pasted up on one of the windows.

Hamish pushed open the door and went in. It was a monument to the age of plastic: plastic plants trailed plastic fronds from plastic flower-boxes; plastic-covered chairs crouched beside low plastic tables. Even the long bar was made of plastic painted to look like wood. Hamish asked the barman for an orange juice and was mildly surprised to receive it in a glass tumbler instead of a plastic beaker. It was ten in the morning. A few couples were seated at the tables eating Mullen's Breakfast Special. Perhaps, thought Hamish, it was livelier in the evenings, with bands and crowds.

"Have you got Johnny Rankin and the Stotters playing here?" asked Hamish. "I don't see them on the bill."

"No' this month," said the barman. "Maybe next."

"I've never heard of any of the groups you've got advertised," said Hamish.

"Aye, weel, the manager books the cheap acts, that's why. Some of them are chronic."

"Could I hae a word with the manager?"

"Who's asking?"

"Police," said Hamish patiently, pointing to his uniform.

"Whit, again? Hang on a minute and I'll see if Mr. Mullen's aboot."

Hamish waited patiently. One customer shuffled

over to the juke-box and dropped in some coins. Soon a pleasant tenor voice filled the room, singing "Over the Sea to Skye," conjuring up Jacobite romance, far from the reality of this plastic road house.

A small squat hairy man appeared behind the bar. He had very black eyes, like stones, and odd tufts of hair on his face, and hair sprouting from his nostrils and ears. He looked like a troglodyte squeezed into twentieth-century clothing.

"Mullen," he said curtly to Hamish by way of introduction. "What d'ye want?"

"I want to talk to you about Cheryl Higgins," said Hamish.

"Oh, her! What can I tell you that I've no' said a'ready? She was here all right from nine till one in the morning, caterwauling away."

"And you're sure it was her?"

"If you can find another lassie in the Highlands wi' thon orange hair, it'll be a miracle. No, it was her all right. Foul-mouthed creature, but then a lot of them are."

"And she didn't leave the room at any time during the show?"

"Naw, that lot are like camels. Once they've got an audience, they can go on for hours and hours."

Hamish thanked him and left, feeling depressed.

But he got into the police Land Rover and drove off in the direction of the travellers' campsite.

As he parked outside the field, he noticed the flurry of activity the sight of him caused. Weird figures were seen scuttling here and there, doors banged shut as children were scooped up and carried inside. It was as if a monster had arrived, but Hamish guessed they were probably hiding drugs or items of petty theft.

Only one woman stayed where she was, stirring something in a cooking-pot over an open fire.

Hamish approached her. "Where are the Stoddarts?" he asked. She was a thin, fantastically dressed creature, wearing a heather coronet on her tangled locks. A long Indian cotton dress hung about with beads and brooches was wrapped around her body. She turned pale dim eyes up to him and frowned as if he had asked her to expound Einstein's Theory of Relativity. "The Stoddarts," he prompted.

"Ower there," she said, pointing in the direction of a small caravan painted bright blue.

Hamish walked up to it and knocked on the door. A vague-looking bearded man answered it.

"Mr. Stoddart," said Hamish, "is Cheryl Higgins here?"

"Come in," he said and retreated back into the dimness of the caravan, which still had its curtains drawn closed. The confined space smelled of unwashed bodies. The bearded man joined a slattern of a girl, no doubt his wife, at a table at one end. Both were watching television on a small black-and-white set placed on the table. Hamish looked round. At the other end of the caravan was a bunk with a flaming-orange head poking above the pile of bed-clothes. He went over.

"Cheryl," he said.

She twisted round and looked up at him. Then her mouth opened and a stream of abuse poured out. Hamish waited patiently until she had run dry, guessing correctly that Cheryl's outpourings were part of a long-established pattern.

When she fell silent, he perched on the end of the bed and said quietly, "Now you've got that out of your system, I want to ask questions about you and Sean, not the usual ones."

She gazed at him sullenly.

"Why did you leave Sean?" asked Hamish.

"It wasnae any kind o' life," she said bitterly. "I think he wus screwed in the heid. He would get visits from thae awful old women frae the village and ask me to take a walk and sometimes I couldnae get back to ma bed till after midnight."

Hamish felt suddenly miserable. He did not want to ask any further questions but knew he had to.

"Who were these women?"

As if she sensed that he didn't really want to know, Cheryl brightened visibly and something like a look of satisfaction came into her eyes. "Well, there was that fat Wellington cow, for one. 'Dear Sean, I've just baked this cake specially for you.' Ugh. Then there was a wee wumman wi' glasses who sounded like a jammed record." Jessie Currie, thought Hamish. "Aye, and the doctor's wife, too."

"Anyone else?"

"Isn't that enough?"

"How often did Sean beat you?"

She sat up in bed and hugged her thin arms about her body. "Get oot o' here," she muttered.

"All right, I'll leave that question aside for the moment. Have you any idea what the relationship between Sean and these women was?"

"It couldnae hae been sex," she jeered. "He strung them along so he could get presents o' food and cakes."

"Money?" asked Hamish sharply, remembering the missing hundred pounds.

"No," she mumbled, her head going down again.

He tried and tried but Cheryl said she had nothing more to tell. As far as she knew, Sean enjoyed causing a flutter among the middle-aged women of the village, and yet Sean must have done something wrong, for after his death no one had a good word to say for him.

Hamish finally gave up and left. He stood outside the caravan and looked slowly around at the other caravans and ancient buses which were dotted about the field. He felt sad and weary and so had a sudden understanding of why these unlovely people stepped out of society and took to the road. No responsibilities, no rent, no jobs, unless playing the occasional gig could be called a job. No hard drugs; drink, glue, or hashish when they could get it. They helped each other out, romanticized their life-style, and often got other people to believe in that romance. Let other people pay the taxes to supply them with dole money, let other people build and maintain the roads they drove on, let other people clean up the mess they left behind; they were the Peter Pans who had found a way of never growing out of adolescence, and the rest of the world was one indulgent parent to see to their needs.

A small fine rain was scudding in on a warm west wind. The woman was still stirring that pot, although the fire had blown out. Hamish gave himself a mental shake. It was unlike him to stand moralizing in the middle of a damp field when he himself was hardly one of the world's exemplary workers.

So what had Sean done with the women? he wondered as he drove north again. Had he talked them into some sort of mental crisis, like the one he had inflicted on the minister? He had undoubtedly possessed a certain magnetism. But what had he done to drive someone to bashing his face and head in? It had been a murder done in pure hatred.

Mrs. Wellington, Angela Brodie, and Jessie Currie would have to be questioned again, and this time without their minders: Mrs. Wellington without the minister, Angela without Dr. Brodie and Jessie without Nessie.

Evening was settling down on Lochdubh as he drove down the hill in the heathery twilight. The fishing boats were setting out to sea. Smoke rose lazily from chimneys and a group of children were playing on the beach, their cries as shrill as the calls of sea-birds. But the blackness, the malignancy that lay under it all would never go away unless he found out who had murdered Sean.

He went into the police station, thinking wryly that for all his impatience with Willie, he was becoming spoilt by being perpetually waited on.

But Willie was in the living-room slumped in front of a television set. "Where did that come from?" asked Hamish.

"Mr. Ferrari," said Willie dully. "It's an auld one o' his. He's got one of the new ones. This one disnae have the remote control."

"That's grand," said Hamish. "What's on?"

"I dinnae know and I dinnae care. I don't like television."

Hamish sat down opposite him, first turning off the set.

"Out with it, Willie."

"It's a serious matter and I don't want tae have to put up with your usual levitation."

"No levity, I promise."

"I was at the restaurant," began Willie.

"You're always at that restaurant," said Hamish impatiently.

Willie threw him a hurt look.

"I'm sorry," said Hamish quickly. "What happened? Was it anything to do with Lucia?"

Willie nodded.

"Did you make a pass at her and get your face slapped?"

Willie sat up straight. "I would never lay a finger on that lassie if she didnae want it."

"So what's the problem?"

"I shouldnae hae been listening," said Willie. "Lucia said there was a new dish the cook, Luigi, wanted me to try. It was this morning and the restaurant wasn't opened yet. So I was sitting at the table over by that auld fireplace and I could hear Mr. Ferrari quite clearly. He was talking to someone in the room above, a man. I heard the name Sean Gourlay and that's when I started to listen.

"Mr. Ferrari said, 'Thon bastard's dead and gone, thank goodness. I'm glad I was saved from killing him myself.' The other man said something I couldnae hear and then Mr. Ferrari said, 'After what he did to Lucia...' And then I couldnae hear any mair."

"So did you ask him about it?"

"I couldnae," wailed Willie. "If there was something between her and thon monster, I don't want tae know."

"I'm beginning to think not knowing iss worse than anything else," said Hamish, half to himself. "Help yourself to a whisky, Willie. I'll ask Ferrari."

"He'll know I was listening!" cried Willie.

"True, but I'll tell him you couldn't help it."

As Hamish walked along to the restaurant, he turned over the names of the staff in his mind. There was old Mr. Ferrari, and Lucia, who acted as waitress. Conchita Gibson, another distant relative who had married a Scotsman who had died of cancer the year before; Luigi, the cook; Giovanni, the undercook; and Mrs. Maclean, Archie the fisherman's wife, who came in daily to clean, made up the rest of the staff.

The restaurant was fairly busy, for its reputation had grown so much that many of the customers motored long distances to eat there and the prices were still low enough to tempt the locals.

Lucia welcomed Hamish with a dazzling smile. She really is a stunner, thought Hamish. Poor Willie. Not a hope in hell.

He asked for Mr. Ferrari. Lucia disappeared and then returned and led him through the back of the restaurant and up a flight of stairs to the flat over the shop.

"Come in, Sergeant," cried Mr. Ferrari. "Have a drink, but don't stay too long, because I've a lot to attend to."

"No drink," said Hamish, "chust a few questions. Willie was here this morning."

"Grand lad, that. Should be in the restaurant trade."

"Maybe. The fact is he wass sitting next to the fireplace and he could hear something of what you were saying upstairs."

All the wrinkles on Mr. Ferrari's old face settled into a sort of hard mask from behind which his eyes peered warily out.

"All he could gather," Hamish went on, "wass that you were glad someone had killed Sean or you might have done it yourself after what he did to Lucia. Now who were you talking to and what did Sean Gourlay do to Lucia?"

"Like the television set?" asked Mr. Ferrari.

"If that wass meant as a bribe, then you can be having it back!" exclaimed Hamish. Mr. Ferrari looked at Hamish steadily.

"Don't you see you are making matters worse for yourself?" said Hamish. "Tell me the truth."

"And you will not tell anyone?" Mr. Ferrari demanded.

"Not unless it's necessary, no."

"It's not a nice story. Lucia does not go out walking with any man without my permission. Sean asked her to go for a walk with him, she asked me and I refused. I did not want her tied to anyone who showed no signs of wanting to work. But he was a regular customer, although where he got the money from, I don't know, and so he managed to speak to her . . . a lot. He was very handsome. So Lucia begged and begged to be allowed to go out with him, so I at last said she could on her day off, in the afternoon, but she was to be back at six o'clock. I sent Giovanni after them to keep watch. I tell you, Hamish," he went on, "I've met a lot of bad people in my long life, and I had Sean marked down as a real bad one. But I couldn't be sure. I kept wishing that wee lassie, Cheryl, had still been with him. Lucia wouldnae have dreamt of going out with him then.

"So off they went and Giovanni set out after them. All excited he was, dodging in and out of doorways with a cap down over his eyes and a scarf over his mouth, and then creeping up the hillside. I thought Sean was bound to notice the idiot, but as it turned out, he did not.

"They only went a little away up on the moor and they were sitting side by side on one of those big boulders. Giovanni crept up and lay in the heather behind them.

"Sean began telling Lucia she was the most beautiful woman he'd ever seen and she asked if he'd been in love with Cheryl and he gave her a spiel that Cheryl was a waif frae Glasgow he was being kind to and what had bit the hand that fed it and all that rubbish.

"Then he suggested she go back to that bus of his. He said he had some good videos. But she said it was their first time out and wasn't the view lovely and maybe another time and so on. Then he grabbed her and kissed her and Giovanni said he didn't know what to do because she was enjoying it and it was only kissing. Then Sean began to unbutton her blouse and Lucia pushed him off, but he tumbled her onto the ground and I believe Giovanni when he said it could have been rape if he hadn't been there. So Giovanni ups from the heather and shouts, 'Stop!'

"He said Sean looked like the very devil, those cat's eyes of his glittering in the light, and Lucia, she was crying her eyes out. Giovanni said he was right glad he'd taken the meat cleaver with him."

Hamish suppressed a grin.

"So Sean saw that cleaver and began to run and Giovanni went after him and chased him right back to that bus. Then he told me. So we all went to see him, me and Luigi and Giovanni, and we told Sean Gourlay that if he came near the restaurant or Lucia ever again, we would cut his balls off. So that's it."

"You should have told me this before," said Hamish.

"Why?" demanded Mr. Ferrari. "None of us killed him."

But Hamish left very worried. There was a field at the back of the restaurant and from the field it was possible to cut across the other fields and get to the one behind the manse. And yet how simple it would be for him if, say, Giovanni had done it. How he longed for an outsider. And yet, although Mr. Ferrari and his relatives had only set up their restaurant a short time ago in the village, they had quickly become a valuable part of the local life. The small shack which served as a Catholic church was to be gradually replaced by a brick building, money supplied by Mr. Ferrari. The restaurant had become a gathering place for local birthdays and wedding anniversaries.

At the police station, he told Willie what had

happened. "I should've been there," said Willie. "Not that Lucia cannae protect herself."

"In what way?"

"She told me she was walking home and one o' the forestry lads grabbed her and tried to steal a kiss."

"And?"

"She kicked him in the family silver."

"You mean jewels."

"Whatever."

Could Lucia have done it herself? wondered Hamish. She had been keen enough on Sean to beg Mr. Ferrari to let her go out with him. Was she one of the women who had gone to the bus? Cheryl wouldn't know, for Sean's pursuit of Lucia had started after Cheryl had gone.

He shook his head wearily. "Did Mr. Ferrari blame me for reporting it?" asked Willie anxiously.

Hamish shook his head. "As long as you go on neglecting your duties and giving him free labour, he won't go off you."

"It's not as if anything ever happens in Lochdubh," said Willie sulkily.

"Except murder," said Hamish.

Hamish set out the next day to try to get his female suspects alone. He waited until he knew Dr. Brodie would be at the surgery and went to call on Angela. He felt a

pang of worry when he saw her. It was like that time
when that woman had been murdered in Lochdubh, he
thought, and Angela, who had been under her influence, had mentally gone off the rails. She looked now
as she had then, thin and brittle.

"Not more questions," said Angela when she saw
him.

"I have to keep asking," said Hamish patiently. "Can
I come in?"

"I suppose so." Angela led the way into the kitchen.
The table was covered in textbooks. She shovelled
a clear space at one corner and sat down. Hamish sat
opposite her.

"I went to see Cheryl yesterday," said Hamish.
Angela pushed a tress of fine wispy hair out of her eyes.
"And?" she demanded.

"I gather that some evenings, Cheryl was sent out for
a walk while Sean entertained some ladies. You were
one of the ones mentioned. The previous times I've spoken to you, you've always said you went over with cakes
and things when Sean and Cheryl originally came to the
village, as a sort of welcome. You never said anything
about spending any time with Sean alone."

"I didn't want my husband to find out," said Angela.
"All that happened was that I went over one evening
to talk about my studies because he had seemed interested, and John never listens to me. When I talk about
anything to do with this Open University degree, he

switches off. Cheryl went out when I arrived. I stayed and talked, had a few drinks and then left. I never went back again because I thought if John ever found out about it, it would... well... look odd."

"And that's all there was to it?"

"Yes, Hamish, what else could there have been?"

"Sean didn't ask you for money or..." Hamish looked at her in growing concern "...drugs?"

"I thought you were a friend, Hamish. How can you say such things?" Angela covered her thin face with her thin hands and began to cry.

"Now, now," said Hamish awkwardly. "Dinnae greet. I haff to ask these questions, you know that. Haven't you anything you'd like to get off your chest?"

"I'd like you to get out of here, *now*," yelled Angela, her tear-stained face contorted.

Hamish rose to his feet and stood looking down at her. "I'll go now," he said heavily, "but I'll have to be back."

Priscilla, he thought, as he stood outside the doctor's house, I need Priscilla. He drove up to the hotel in time to catch her closing up the gift shop for lunch.

"Hullo, Hamish," she said, "I'm just about to have lunch, coffee and sandwiches in the bar. You can join me, if you'd like."

When they were seated in a corner of the bar, Hamish having agreed to coffee and refused whisky because he was driving, much as he would have liked one, for he had found the interview with Angela harrowing, Priscilla looked at him and said, "This case is really getting you down. Want to talk about it?"

So he told her all he knew from the beginning, outlining his fear that the murder had been committed by someone from the village.

"I think we should write some of this down," said Priscilla. She rose and went through to the reception desk and came back with several sheets of paper. "Now," she said, "let's sort it out. All the women who have visited Sean have become wrecks. Mrs. Wellington is a shadow of her former self. Angela is on the twitch and spending far too much money on clothes, which is totally out of character. The Currie sisters plan to sell up and move. Sean dies. They take the sign down.

"There's a common factor there, Hamish. You're normally so acute. You've missed it although it's been staring you in the face all the time because you're praying for some outsider to turn out to be the murderer."

"And what's the common factor?"

Priscilla tapped the paper with her pen.

"Money," she said. "They all needed money. Perhaps not Mrs. Wellington. But the rest badly needed money."

Chapter Seven

☠

O villain, villain, smiling, damned villain!

—Shakespeare

Hamish looked down at the paper, his mind scurrying this way and that, trying to find a road away from the three women.

Then he gave a sigh and leaned back. "Aye, you're maybe right. But Angela now, she was spending money on *herself*, not Sean."

Priscilla tapped the paper again. "Drugs, Hamish. The missing morphine. And there's another thing."

"What's that?"

"I called on Angela. She was wearing a black dress. I complimented her on it although I thought it made her look like a waiflike widow and she said uneasily that it had cost an awful lot of money, that it was a Dior."

"So was it?"

"Yes, I should think it was—but a second-hand Dior."

"How second-hand?"

"There were worn patches under the arms and although it was a simple style, it's very short in the skirt and I would guess it was about twenty years old."

"What are you getting at?"

"There are thrift shops in Inverness, Hamish, where a woman can buy a model dress for a few pounds and then tell her husband it cost a fortune."

Hamish looked at her miserably.

"Now, Hamish, it may not be any of them, but you'll never get to the bottom of it if you don't start finding out why they all needed money. Sean must have been blackmailing them."

"And Sean is dead and they're all still worried, although the Currie sisters have decided to stay in Lochdubh," said Hamish. "And they are worried, which means they think perhaps Cheryl or someone might have got their hands on the blackmailing material. I'm going back for another look at that bus."

"I notice it's still there," said Priscilla. "Wasn't there a mother or someone who was going to claim it?"

"Yes. Mrs. Gourlay. She said she would be up next week to take a few things. She asked if anyone would want to buy the bus and I suggested she try Ian Chisholm at the garage. I'd better start work right away."

"Could Willie help?"

"I doubt it. He's really lovesick now. Lucia's walking out with Tim Queen."

"Oh, dear," said Priscilla. Tim Queen was a handsome young man whose father owned the Lochdubh Bar.

"Aye, Willie skulks around after them, looking like a whipped dog."

Walking out was an old-fashioned pastime, but there was little else for a courting couple to do in Lochdubh. Lucia and Tim Queen were leaning over the bridge, looking down at the River Anstey. Lucia kept flicking little speculative looks at Tim from under her long lashes. He was tall and red-haired, with a square, pleasant freckled face. The Lochdubh Bar, once an extension of the Lochdubh Hotel, which was still awaiting a buyer, had been bought by Tim's father in a separate sale and had been making a profit ever since.

Tim looked down at Lucia's small red hands, which were resting on the parapet of the bridge, and then covered one of them with his own. Lucia snatched her hand away.

"What's the matter?" asked Tim. "I was only holding your hand."

"I am ashamed of my hands," said Lucia, putting them behind her back. "They are so red. I would like soft white hands."

"But that's what I like about ye," said Tim earnestly. "You're an old-fashioned girl. I don't like the young ones round here who slap paint all ower their faces and never do a day's work and wouldnae know how to scrub a kitchen floor if you asked them."

Lucia's beautiful eyes became clouded with sad thought. "So you like a woman who does the housework, Teem?"

He slid an arm about her waist. "Yes, that's my sort of girl. My friend, Johnny, over at Darquhart, just got married, and his wife, Darleen, well, she wanted a cleaning woman frae day one!"

"What is so odd about that?"

He laughed. "You silly wee thing, why should Johnny pay for a cleaning woman when he's got a wife?"

She slid out from his arm and looked about. "Why, there is Constable Lamont," she cried.

She was looking at a stand of trees beside the river. Tim could not see anything.

But Lucia waved and sure enough, Willie eased out from behind a tree. "Do not bother to walk back with me, Teem," said Lucia gaily. "See, I am safe with my policeman."

And Tim never knew what he had said wrong.

Hamish collected the keys to the bus from the police station and then strode up to the field behind the manse. Sean's presence still seemed to be around the place. He had a superstitious feeling that he was still in the bus and would laugh at him when he opened the door.

The day was warm and overcast, with great clouds of midges dancing on the muggy air.

He unlocked the door of the bus and climbed inside.

Everything was as the forensic team had left it and as he had last seen it. He began to search methodically, but wondering all the time what he could find that an experienced forensic team had missed. He even opened packets of coffee and bags of sugar in the hope of discovering something hidden in them. He worked for hours and did not find one thing.

He sat down miserably on a bench at the side of the table and looked dully at the blank screen of the small television set. There were videos piled up in a heap at the end of the table. As a last hope, he slid them out of their packets. They were mostly of the brutal-sex-and-violence kind, but nothing under the counter, nothing illegal. He sighed. Then suddenly a little picture came into his brain, a picture of Sean striding along the waterfront with that easy athletic pace of his, carrying a video camera. He looked wildly around. There was the television, there were the videos, there was the video recorder, but no camera. But Patel rented one out.

The bus was still hitched up to the manse electricity. He switched on the television set and began to feed the videos into the machine, fast-forwarding them through a series of murders and rapes and general mayhem. The weather was clearing outside and yellow sunlight suddenly flooded the interior of the bus. Children's voices drifted in along with the other homely sounds of the village, a different world from the misery of filth and violence which was flickering in front of him.

He ejected the one he had scanned through and put in another called *The Rage of the Mutants* and pressed the fast-forward button. Then, with an exclamation, he ran it back to the beginning and began to play it at normal speed. With a sinking heart, he found himself looking at Mrs. Wellington. She was smoking and giggling and drinking. Hamish stopped the film and peered hard at that cigarette. It was a reefer, hash, grass. "You do make me feel wicked," Mrs. Wellington burbled as he started the film again. Her eyes were glazing over. Sean's voice was only a mumble in the background. Then there was a long blank and suddenly a couple in an amorous embrace leaped onto the screen. Angela Brodie and Sean. His mouth was clamped over hers and one hand was stroking her breast and she was moaning in his embrace. Angela suddenly pulled free and the film went blank again. It ran on towards the end and then Hamish blushed. For there was Jessie Currie, stark-naked, roaring and laughing and holding a glass of something. And then the film finished.

Hamish sat back, sweating. It all fell into place: Mrs. Wellington's distress and the missing money from the Mothers' Union, Angela and the second-hand dress and the missing morphine, Jessie and Nessie selling their house.

He should phone Strathbane and send them the video and let them take it from there. But he could not. Even if none of them had murdered Sean, their reputations would be in rags. Dr. Brodie and Mr. Wellington would have to know what their wives had been up to.

Hamish switched off the television set and put everything back in place, except the incriminating video, which he took with him. There must be some way round this. For a start, he would have to try to get the culprits alone.

He let himself out of the bus and carefully locked the door. He stood blinking in the late sunshine. A brisk wind was blowing and the midges had gone.

He had a sudden picture of Sean, smiling and lounging beside the bus, his hands thrust into his trouser pockets, and Hamish Macbeth felt that he could have murdered the man himself for wrecking such innocence. Hamish was sure Cheryl either did not know about the money or, if she had, had not been able to get any of it. If that was the case, it still had to be hidden somewhere. He looked slowly around. There was no outside toilet, and none on the bus. Sean had probably used one of the lavatories at the manse, the one situated just inside the back door. There was nothing outside except the packing case lying on its side, gaping empty, on which Sean and Cheryl had sat on the day he had come to search for morphine. He gave it a slight push and then peered inside. It was weighted down with rocks.

He placed the video carefully on the grass and crawled inside the packing case and dragged out the rocks. Then he pushed it aside. A square patch of bleached grass was revealed. He examined it closely and noticed that the square was made up of squares of long-grassed turf. Excited, he started to haul them up; a difficult job, for they had begun to grow together. Finally he got the last one clear and smiled with satisfaction. Buried underneath was a plastic garbage bag full of something. He pulled it up and opened it. It was heavy but proved to be weighted with stones. But inside as well was a square cash box. The box was locked. "Tampering with the evidence," screamed a voice of warning in his head, but he shrugged it away and took out a set of skeleton keys from his pocket and got to work. It took some time and he was glad the bus screened him from the manse windows. Finally the lock clicked and he opened the lid. The box was stuffed with pound notes—fifties, twenties, tens and fives. Underneath lay four packets of morphine. He counted the money carefully. Just over a thousand pounds. Hardly blackmail on a grand scale. He carefully replaced everything and put the bag back in the hole and covered it over with the turf and the packing case and then crawled inside to replace the rocks. Once the rocks were pushed to the back, he realized that to the forensic team, they would not be visible and it would have simply looked to them like an empty packing case on its side, showing the world that there was nothing there.

He consoled himself with the thought that he could always pretend to find the stuff later. Right now, he meant to confront the women on that video. But how to get them alone?

Two days later, Angela Brodie opened a thin envelope and stared mesmerized at the thin typewritten slip inside. It said, "Come to the police station at ten this morning. I have a film to show you. Hamish Macbeth."

"What's that?" asked Dr. Brodie. "You look as if you've seen a ghost."

"Nothing," said Angela. "I thought it was my exam results and got all upset, but it's just a note from Mrs. Wellington. There's to be a meeting at the church hall to discuss raising funds."

"Hope nobody pinches them again," said the doctor, losing interest.

Mrs. Wellington at that same moment was reading a note from Hamish Macbeth. She let out a squawk and her husband lowered his newspaper and looked at her impatiently. "Another bill?" he asked.

"No, it's nothing," she said, crushing the envelope and slip of paper in her large hand. "Some Mothers' Union business. I've got to go out this morning."

But the minister was once more reading his newspaper and did not seem to care.

Nessie Currie twitched the slip of paper out of her sister Jessie's trembling fingers.

"I'm ruined . . . ruined," whispered Jessie.

"You'll need to face up to him," said Nessie. "I'll come with you."

"No, no. I'll need to go on my own, on my own. Everyone will find out, find out. I cannae stay here."

"You have sinned against the Lord," said Nessie, "and you must take your punishment." Then her face softened. "I'll come along as well, Jessie. I'll stand by you. We'll face this together, and then we'll sell up and go far down south, Inverness or somewhere like that."

Willie, delighted to have a morning off, had actually offered to take Towser for a walk. He had finally taken an odd liking to Hamish's yellowish mongrel of a dog, mainly because Lucia liked Towser and Towser had developed a taste for pasta.

Hamish had borrowed a video recorder from Mr. Patel, not wanting to borrow the one from the bus in case anyone saw him with it and asked him what he was doing. Angela, Mrs. Wellington and the Currie sisters arrived together.

Hamish silently ushered them into the living-room, where they sat down with jerky movements, and all stared mesmerized at the still blank television screen.

Hamish slid the cassette into the recorder. He ran the film. When it had finished, he looked at them. Angela and Mrs. Wellington were sitting together on the sofa, and they were holding hands. Nessie had an arm around Jessie's shoulders. But despite their distress and obvious strain, there was a faint air of surprised relief about them all. They were not alone, he realized, in their misery and shame, and that was the reason for the faint air of relief.

"The situation is this," said Hamish. "I have found the money and the morphine, but I cannot do anything about returning it. I should be down in Strathbane showing this video at headquarters. The reason I have not done so should be obvious to all of you. For some reason you let this man trick you and blackmail you. The only way out of it is to try to find the murderer and get the case closed."

"But if you find the murderer," said Angela in a croaky voice, "it will all come out in court and the video will be shown as well."

"Not necessarily. I am in as bad trouble as the rest of you, for I could easily lose my job for suppressing this evidence. If I find the murderer, it is possible I can do a deal. I will promise him or her not to mention the blackmailing so that charge will not be added on to the one of murder. But I'll never find out who murdered Sean unless everyone here tells the truth." He turned to Angela. "You first."

She pushed her wispy hair back from her eyes. "It was a sort of madness," she said. "He was so handsome. He made it clear that he had no interest in Cheryl, other than giving her a home, and I believed him. He was so interested in this degree I am studying for, the only person who has ever shown any interest."

Except me, who pushed you into doing it, thought Hamish huffily.

"It was easy to forget Cheryl," went on Angela, "because as soon as I arrived, she went out. I'd never even looked at any other man since I married John. Oh, I was flattered that such a young and good-looking man seemed to find me attractive. If he'd come on too strong at the beginning, I would have shied away, but I am very romantic and he used the romantic approach. He asked me to come one evening and said he had some films to show me. I told John I was going to see Mrs. Wellington. Instead of any films, he produced a bottle of champagne. I'm not used to drinking—I had told him that—and I got drunk pretty quickly. We were sitting on that bench at the end of the bus. He began to kiss me and I...responded. And then I heard this whirring sound, very faint, and I looked down the bus and I could see the video camera propped on the table facing us and I realized it was running. I pushed him away and stumbled out of that bus and ran home and I vowed never to go near him again. I only thought he was weird because he was prepared to film our love-making without telling me.

"He stopped me in the street a few days later. He said he would show the film to my husband unless I paid him. John and I have a joint account. I panicked and said I couldn't. He laughed and told me to get him some morphine and then he would leave me alone.

"I took the keys to the surgery that night when John was asleep and got the drugs. I thought that would be an end of it, but next week he was back, asking for money. I was frantic with worry. He said he didn't want much. At first he asked for fifty, then it was a hundred, then another hundred, and so on. I pretended to John that I was buying expensive dresses in Inverness and paying cash for them when in fact I was buying them cheap from the thrift shops. I was so glad when I heard he was dead and then, when I realized the police would probably find that video, I was frightened to death all over again. Oh, Hamish, John must never find out."

"I'll do my best," said Hamish heavily. He faced Jessie. "Now you."

Jessie sobbed and stumbled over the words and repeated everything, but the sad story slowly emerged. She, too, had been flattered by the attentions of this young man. She had gone to the bus. He gave her something to drink and she didn't remember a thing after that until somehow she was in her own bed at home and Nessie was sitting next to her.

"He must have put something in her drink," said Nessie, "for she was raving and seeing things. I didnae call the doctor, thank the Lord for that, for I thought she maybe had the DTs and that would have been a shame and disgrace. When she told me she had had one drink and didn't remember anything after that, I didnae believe her. Then Sean Gourlay called, as bold as brass. He asked to see her alone. After he had gone, I could see she was frightened to death and so I got it out of her. He wanted twenty pounds. That's a lot for us. Dad left us the house and a bit in the bank, but just enough for us to get by on if we watch carefully. I told Jessie to give him the twenty but warned her he would probably be back. And so he was. So I said to Jessie we should sell up and get out of Lochdubh where he could never find us..." Her voice trailed off and she sat in dumb misery.

Oh, may you burn in hell, Sean Gourlay, thought Hamish. Jessie was probably, at the age of fifty-something, still a virgin. She and Nessie were staunch church-goers. No one would ever think, looking at the pair of them, that there would ever be anything about either of them to blackmail. They both had brown hair, permed ferociously into small tight curls, and thick glittering glasses and thin spare figures.

"Now, Mrs. Wellington," he said, "what is your story?"

"He said they were Turkish cigarettes," said Mrs.

Wellington bitterly. "And how would I know any different? He made me feel young and reckless and I had *never* felt young or reckless before. I haven't even any children." Hamish did not feel like asking her what she meant by that. "I married a suitable man and settled down to do good works. I was tired of good works," she said, tears starting to her eyes, "and now look what my wickedness has brought me to. I'm a silly old fool. I, like Mrs. Brodie, have a joint account, and Mr. Wellington checks it every week!" Hamish had always considered it odd that Mrs. Wellington always referred to her husband as "Mr. Wellington," like a Victorian lady. "I was so desperate, I thought if I gave him a big sum, he would go away. He *promised* to go away. I stole the money from the Mothers' Union. But he came back for more. I sold some of my jewellery to keep him quiet. When he died, I was so glad it was all over."

"And did any of you kill him?" asked Hamish.

"No," said Mrs. Wellington.

"No," squeaked Jessie.

"I wanted to," said Angela heavily. "I dreamt about it every day. But I didn't kill him. What happens now, Hamish?"

"I'll need to keep this evidence here, in my room where Willie won't find it, and then try to see Cheryl again. She must have known about the blackmailing. She knew what she was doing when she went out for those walks and left Sean alone with one or other of you."

"Surely she murdered him," said Angela.

"I would like to think that," sighed Hamish. "But at the time of the murder she was performing with a pop group in front of witnesses, and I cannae break her alibi. Keep quiet, all of you, and we might come out of this. But if I find one of you killed Sean Gourlay, then there will be no more covering anything up. I've got a week. In a week's time, Sean's mother comes up here to take away a few things and try to sell the bus. Of course, I could always put the video with the other things I found," he added half to himself.

"You mean you found the missing drugs?" asked Angela eagerly.

"And the money?" put in Mrs. Wellington.

"Yes."

"Where?" asked Angela. "Can't we have the money back, and the drugs?"

"No, I'm sorry. They'll have to stay where they are for now."

When the women had gone, Hamish went through to the office and made notes, writing down what he knew, but without seeing any glimmer of hope.

The phone beside him rang. It was a tearful woman calling to say a truck had crashed into her car up on the moors. He drove off to deal with that but all the while his mind was turning over what he knew and worrying in case one of the three women was a murderess.

It was during that evening when the light began to

fade and Willie was whistling to himself in the kitchen as he prepared the supper that Hamish, with a sudden lurch in his stomach, wondered if any of the three might go to the bus to try to find the money or drugs.

He shouted to Willie that he had to go out and to keep his dinner warm and made his way up to the manse field. The bus stood dark and forlorn. Hamish crouched down behind the packing case, deciding to give it an hour or so. Mrs. Wellington and Angela, if they wanted to make a move, would do so before bedtime so as not to rouse their husbands' suspicions by getting up and going out in the middle of the night.

By eleven o'clock he was beginning to shiver, for the night was getting cold. He rose stiffly up from behind the packing case and then crouched down again. Three shadowy figures were at the edge of the field. He waited a moment and then switched on the large torch he was carrying, stood up and shone it straight at the bus. Angela, Mrs. Wellington and Jessie Currie swung round and stood hypnotized in the light like startled rabbits.

Hamish walked towards them. Angela was carrying a hammer, no doubt to break the lock.

"I know what you're after," said Hamish severely, "and you're not getting it. Now, I'm going out on a limb and putting my job on the line for the lot of ye. The least you can all do iss not to try to tamper wi' the evidence more than it's been tampered with already. Off tae your beds, ladies, and if I see just one of you near this bus again I'll take the whole lot, video and all, and let Strathbane see it."

They shuffled off silently, without a word.

Hamish followed them just as slowly. He was haunted by the sight of Angela holding that hammer. You think you know people so well, and when something like murder happens you realize you really don't know much about them at all. Angela had previously proved herself to be unstable, but the circumstances had been stressful. Mrs. Wellington he had believed to be the sort of character of a Good Woman that she presented to the world, and Jessie and Nessie he had regarded affectionately as a couple of jokes. He must try Cheryl again.

Next morning, he told Willie he wanted the day off and asked him to look after things. Hamish cynically noticed his dog, who would normally have been scrabbling at the Land Rover, was happy to be left behind. Towser had been seduced by Willie's cooking.

He took Willie's battered Ford instead of the police car, not wanting to advertise his presence in Strathbane to anyone from headquarters.

The farther he drove from Lochdubh, the more he felt like an irresponsible fool. He should never have become so involved with the locals in a murder inquiry. He should have phoned Strathbane, told them about the new evidence, and let them take it from there. For all he knew of them, Mrs. Wellington, Angela, or even Jessie Currie might be capable of murder.

If only Cheryl hadn't so many witnesses. He would no doubt find her again and she would swear and curse and he would get nothing more out of her. He could not tell her about the video without risking exposing the three women.

It was all so hopeless.

He was approaching Mullen's Roadhouse. He slowed down. A large new poster was pinned up on the window. Top of the bill was Johnny Rankin and the Stotters. He stopped the car and climbed out. They were due to perform that evening.

He decided to phone Willie and say he would be in Strathbane until very late. He had to see that performance and judge if there was any way Cheryl might have managed to slip out. She had that scooter. But it would take about two hours surely to get to Lochdubh, park the scooter outside the village, go to the bus on foot, murder Sean, and then get back.

He was turning the problem over in his mind when a slim figure on a scooter shot past. Under the crash helmet he could see the driver had bright-orange hair.

Cheryl!

He set off in pursuit, wishing he were in the Land Rover, wishing he could switch on the siren. The scooter had been painted bright pink and the license plate was obscured by dirt, but there could not be more than one person in the Highlands with that colour of hair. The figure on the scooter glanced back and then simply swerved off the road on a forestry track and sped through the tall thin pine trees. Hamish swung the car off the road, but after only half a mile the track disappeared and ahead he could see that orange hair flitting off through the darkness of the trees.

He cursed under his breath, turned and went back to the road. He would go on to the campsite and confront Cheryl when she arrived.

When he drove into the campsite, that woman was still there, still stirring the pot. As he was not in a police car or in uniform, no one ran away at his arrival. There were fewer old buses and caravans this time, but the bright-blue one belonging to the Stoddarts was still there. He went up and knocked at the door. Again the thin bearded man answered it.

"I would like to wait until Cheryl Higgins returns, Mr. Stoddart," said Hamish.

"Why wait?" he asked amiably and then stood aside. "Help yourself. Herself's in bed as usual."

Chapter Eight

What will not woman, gentle woman dare,
When strong affection stirs her spirit up?

—Robert Southey

The Stoddarts were again watching television. Hamish thought, as he leant over Cheryl to wake her, that he would have expected the Stoddarts to be weaving cloth, painting pictures or doing something artistic rather than watching an Australian soap. They did not seem in the least troubled by his presence.

Cheryl came awake, and as soon as she saw who her visitor was, began her usual litany of oaths and curses. Once he could get a word in, Hamish asked, "Where's your scooter?"

"Whit?"

"You heard."

"I sold it," she said sulkily.

"Who to?"

"Some fella I met in a bar."

"What's his name?"

"I dinnae ken," said Cheryl, shifting restlessly among the frowsty bedclothes. "He gied me cash, I gied him the papers."

"What did he look like?"

"Wee man wi' a leather jacket and black hair."

"Why don't I believe you?" demanded Hamish plaintively. "Were you out this morning?"

"No, I was here in ma bed."

Hamish stood up and approached the Stoddarts. "Was Cheryl out this morning?"

Wayne Stoddart wrenched his eyes from the television screen. "Don't ask me, man," he said. "Only just got up."

Bunty Stoddart, whose face was hidden under a tangled mass of hair, continued to watch and listen avidly to the Australian soap, a vision of sanitized life in the antipodean middle class.

Hamish returned to Cheryl. "I think it was you I chased this morning. There can't be more than two of you in the Highlands with that colour of hair."

Cheryl gave a contemptuous yawn.

Hamish gave up and went outside and began to search around for the scooter. The wind was howling among the piles of refuse and old cars which dotted the field among the buses and caravans. A dismal scene. But there was no sign of the scooter.

He began to experience a pressing nagging fear that

he was in the wrong place, that the clue to the murder lay back in Lochdubh, buried among the inhabitants. But he stubbornly decided to wait in Strathbane until evening and see Johnny Rankin and the Stotters. It was no use questioning Cheryl again. He would not get anything out of her.

He drove into Strathbane, a misery of a place with tall concrete blocks of flats and an air of failure. Nothing had changed. The sea-gulls here seemed dirtier than anywhere else and the oily sea sucked at the rubbish-strewn shore, heaving in on long rolling slow waves, as if exhausted by pollution. He went to the Glen Bar, which he had once frequented when he had been briefly stationed in the town, ordered an orange juice and then sat in a corner and took out a notebook and began to write anything that came into his head about the case.

It slowly dawned on him that he had let his feelings become involved in a dangerous way. Not only was he protecting the three women, he had not questioned Mr. Ferrari thoroughly enough, having let his partiality for hard-working Scottish Italians sway his judgement. Then there was the minister. There was no doubt that the normally scholarly and gentle Mr. Wellington had gone temporarily mad, and the murder had definitely been done by someone in the grip of a murderous rage. Had Mr. Wellington considered *himself* to be the hammer of God?

He had half a mind to call at headquarters and report

the finding of the money, drugs and video and then ask for leave so that he could get away from the village and leave the Strathbane police to do their work.

But perhaps, just perhaps, he might find a clue during the performance of the pop group.

It was a long dreary day and he was glad when evening arrived and he drove to Mullen's Roadhouse, anxious to get it over with.

The huge bar was crowded with a mixture of young people wearing what looked to Hamish like an assortment of jogging suits and staid Scottish couples who had no doubt come because the entertainment was free and there was nothing much else in the way of entertainment in Strathbane.

He was getting tired of orange juice and switched to tomato juice.

There was a small stage in the bar. Various young men were setting up sound equipment and plugging in things and arranging loudspeakers.

At last Johnny Rankin and the Stotters came on. Johnny Rankin was an emaciated young man wearing black leather trousers covered in sequins and nothing else. The only female performer was Cheryl, who was wearing an old-fashioned black corset and black stockings, perhaps hoping to emulate Madonna, although there was something peculiarly sexless about her, but then, reflected Hamish, he had always thought there was something peculiarly sexless about Madonna.

The band swung into action, a hellish cacophony of sound. Cheryl shouted the lyrics and gyrated and twanged a large electric guitar, making up in energy what she so obviously lacked in talent. Strobe lights hurt Hamish's eyes but he kept them fixed on Cheryl. At no time did she leave the stage. He suffered through the whole performance and then went out into the blessed quiet of the night, feeling low. There was no way Cheryl could have left the stage.

He drove back to Lochdubh, regretting that it was now too late to call on Priscilla—Priscilla, who had a marvelous way of clarifying his thoughts. He resolved to see her the next day. The need to turn the evidence over to Strathbane was becoming pressing.

And then, as he was driving past the manse, he suddenly stopped abruptly a little beyond it and looked back up at the field. All the lights were on in the bus. He got out of the car and sprinted up towards the field.

He reached the bus and quietly leaned in through the door. Mr. Wellington, the minister, was feverishly looking through the cupboards. Groceries and Sean's clothes were lying tumbled on the floor.

Hamish stepped inside.

"What the hell do you think you are doing?" he demanded.

Mr. Wellington swung round, his face grey.

"I-I-I lent Sean a v-valuable book," he stammered. "I was looking for it."

"In the middle of the night?" demanded Hamish. "This iss breaking and entering."

"I have a spare set of keys," said Mr. Wellington. "Sean left them at the manse in case he should ever lose his own."

"Then it wass your job to turn them over to the police," snapped Hamish, torn between anxiety and fear. "Do you know what I think? I think you either killed Sean yourself or you think your wife did it."

The minister began to slowly replace everything in the cupboard without speaking.

"I will need to report this," said Hamish heavily.

The minister sat down suddenly on a bench seat at the table and buried his face in his hands. Hamish sat on the bench opposite him. "Tell me what you know," he said gently, "and I will see what I can do to help."

"He was an evil man," muttered the minister. "I thought when he was dead that everything would return to normal. But my wife is still a wreck." He took his hands from his face and looked at Hamish and then gave an odd little sob like a tired child. "You may as well charge me and get it over with, Hamish. I killed him."

Hamish felt deathly tired.

"How?" he asked.

"I took the sledge-hammer and hit him."

"Where?"

"Right here . . . in the bus."

"I don't mean that. I mean, where did you strike him?"

The minister looked at him and then said slowly, "I waited until he had his back to me and then I brought the hammer down on the back of his head."

Hamish felt a wave of relief. "Mr. Wellington, you did not see the body or hear the pathologist's report. The blow that killed him was the very first one and that was a blow to the forehead. Once he was down, the murderer kept on hitting until his head and face were wrecked."

"Yes, yes, that was it," said Mr. Wellington eagerly. "I had forgotten."

"Havers," said Hamish. "You didn't forget because you didn't do it, but you thought your wife did. Why?"

The minister looked defiantly at Hamish and then seemed to collapse. "She was in his bus on the night of the murder," he said.

"What!"

"It was right after the evening service. I saw her walk across. I followed her. I couldn't hear what she was saying but she was crying when she came out. I seized her and demanded to know what was wrong. She became almost hysterical and refused to tell me. I took her indoors and went back. Sean laughed at me and said she had lost her faith as well and was pleading with him to hand it back, just like a book, he said. I tried to punch him, but he was so very strong. He simply picked me up and threw me out onto the grass, laughing his head off.

"I told my wife what he had said and she agreed that

was the case. I suggested we pray together and then she began to laugh at me in a terrible parody of Sean's laughter and told me not to be such an old fool. Later that evening, I heard the back door slam and was sure she had gone back to him again. Perhaps Sean was in love with her. Mrs. Wellington can be a very seductive woman, although she is not aware of it."

Hamish thought of the large and tweedy Mrs. Wellington and blinked.

"Your wife has not been honest with me," he said. "Look, put all the stuff away, lock up and give me the keys. Get your wife out of bed."

But by the time everything was put away, Hamish had decided to leave interviewing Mrs. Wellington until the morning. He said he would call for her and take her along to the police station. If he interviewed her now, he would find it hard to get her alone without the minister. Although his loyalty to the three blackmailed women had been badly shaken, he still did not want to speak to her in front of her husband and so reveal to the minister that his wife was a thief.

Willie was asleep in his room by the time Hamish got home. He went to bed but did not undress. He lay on top of it with Towser at his feet, worrying. Evidence was piling on evidence and he was keeping it all from Strathbane.

He fell into a heavy sleep at dawn and awoke at nine o'clock, all the worries pouring back into his brain. His one thought was to see Priscilla before he interviewed Mrs. Wellington.

"You cannae go out like that," said Willie reprovingly from the kitchen sink. "You've no' shaved and you look as if you've slept in your clothes."

"Haven't time," said Hamish. "Look after Towser for me."

He drove up to the castle. Priscilla was in the office, working at the computer.

"Hamish! What has happened?" she cried. "You look awful."

The door of the office opened and her father came in and bristled at the sight of Hamish. "Shouldn't you be about your duties, officer?" he barked. "I don't want you coming in here and keeping my daughter off her work."

"I've nearly finished," said Priscilla. "Go away, Daddy."

"Show a bit of respect for your father," raged the colonel. "You used to be such a sweet child and you've changed since you came under the pernicious influence of this layabout."

He stormed out.

"Rats," said Priscilla, switching off the computer. "Now he'll be in a foul mood all day. You smell awful, Hamish. Have you started smoking again?"

"No, I was at Mullen's bar last night, and there was enough smoke in there to make an old-fashioned London fog."

"Of course, some normal people change their clothes

from day to day," said Priscilla sweetly. "You'd best come upstairs to my quarters, Hamish, or Daddy will be back to make trouble."

She led him up to the top of the castle, where she had turned two servants' rooms into a bedroom and sitting-room for herself.

Hamish looked around appreciatively. The small room was bright with chintz and flowers and the windows were open to let in the heavy, warm air blowing in from the Gulf Stream. He settled down and told her everything that had happened.

"You are in a mess," commented Priscilla.

"Do you think I should tell Strathbane?"

"My common sense tells me you should tell them everything as quickly as possible, my emotions tell me to keep it all quiet for a bit longer. You're going to have to start questioning everyone all over again. Do you remember when Sean was popular in the village? And then, when he was killed, no one had a good word to say for him? Look at it this way. I think he only directly affected the Curries, the Wellingtons, Cheryl and Angela. But sooner or later that odd sort of Highland telepathy in this village beamed in on the nastiness of the real Sean. Besides, they're quite happy to tolerate some layabout on the dole. They don't like it when the layabout seems to have money to throw around the place on gifts from this shop and meals at the Napoli. So if any man or woman had been up at that bus on the night of the murder as well as Mrs. Wellington, who's going to tell you? Your suspects are desperate to have the murder solved in the hope that their own activities might be covered up, but the villagers would protect one of their own, even if they suspected that person of murder. Mrs. Wellington was at the bus. Maybe *she* saw someone else that evening."

Hamish passed a weary hand over his unshaven face. "You're right. I'd better go."

"Wait and have some coffee and I'll go and borrow an electric razor for you. You've got red bristles."

When she handed him a mug of coffee, Hamish looked at the television set and video in the corner and then at the various remote controls on the table. "I thought you only needed one control," he said, picking one of them up.

"We've got satellite TV now," said Priscilla. "I'll leave you to play with it while I get you that razor. Press 5 on this one and that'll get you satellite TV and then press the various channels on this other one."

Hamish idly switched through the channels, finally ending up with a music one. A thin girl was gyrating to a thudding beat. She was wearing a brief black leather bikini and thigh-length leather boots. "All I gotta say is, screw you, baby," she sang.

"Is that supposed to be sexy?" Hamish asked Priscilla as she came in and handed him a razor.

"Not to you," laughed Priscilla. "That's Jonathan Carty."

"Are you telling me that's a bloke?"

"Yes, a transvestite."

"But he's got boobs!"

"Silicone injections, Hamish. The marvels of modern science."

"Tcha." He switched it off.

"Don't worry, Hamish. The moral revolution's coming. Reaction will set in and even mild womanizers like yourself will be regarded as evil beasts."

"I am not the womanizer," said Hamish. "Where's the bathroom?"

"Along the corridor and on your left. Have a bath while you're at it. I left one of Daddy's clean shirts on the chair in there for you."

"He'll kill you!"

"I really don't take any notice of his rages any more," said Priscilla. "If someone's always raging about something or another, one ceases to listen."

Hamish bathed and shaved and felt considerably better. He said goodbye to Priscilla and drove to the manse and collected Mrs. Wellington despite protests from the minister. Instead of going to the police station, he drove up on the moors and parked off the road on a heathery track.

"Willie's at the station," he said, "and I'm still trying to protect you, but I don't know how long I can go on doing it. I want the whole truth and nothing but the truth. Now, you were at the bus on the night of the murder. When exactly?"

"Nine o'clock," she said in a dull voice.

"Why did you go?"

"I pleaded with him to give me that video. He asked for a thousand pounds. I began to cry. I begged him. I said I could not possibly get that amount of money and he...he laughed at me. I was only there for a few minutes. I realized it was hopeless, so I left. My husband grabbed me outside. He demanded to know what I had been saying, why I had been there, but I could not tell him. Then he returned to the manse later and said Sean had told him I was worried about losing my faith. For one wild moment I felt hope. Sean had not betrayed me. Perhaps he would relent. And then I realized that of course he would not tell my husband the truth while there was still hope of getting money out of me for his silence."

"And you went back out again? Where? Back to the bus?"

Mrs. Wellington hung her head. "I couldn't go back. There were men there."

"Men!" Hamish howled in exasperation. "What men?"

"Mr. Ferrari from the restaurant and two others."

"Good God, woman," raged Hamish, "why did you not tell me this before?"

She raised her head and glared at him with something of her old manner and said distinctly, "Because if they killed him, I was not going to betray them for doing a service for mankind!"

Hamish forced himself to be calm with an effort. "So where did you go?"

"Down on the beach. I walked for a long time, a very long time. I thought of walking into the water and putting an end to the misery, but I could not even find the courage to do that."

"Look," said Hamish urgently, "Mr. Wellington's a Christian minister of the church. It is his duty to forgive. Why don't you tell him?"

"No man is a Christian when it comes to his own wife," she said. "I can't."

"You may have to," warned Hamish. "I'd best see Mr. Ferrari…and you had better start saying your prayers again."

Half an hour later, Hamish was sitting opposite Mr. Ferrari in the flat above the restaurant. It always amazed him that a man who looked so Italian could have such a strong Scottish accent.

"Well, Mr. Ferrari," began Hamish, "I have it on good authority that yourself and two men were up at that bus on the night of the murder." Mr. Ferrari went as still as a lizard on a rock when a shadow crosses it. His old unblinking eyes surveyed Hamish from among the network of brown wrinkles on his face. "I guess the other two men were Luigi and Giovanni," said Hamish.

"That is so," said Mr. Ferrari. He took a small black

cheroot out of a box on a table next to him and lit it carefully.

"Why did you not tell me?" demanded Hamish.

"Because neither of us committed murder, therefore the purpose of our visit was irrelevant," said Mr. Ferrari, blowing a perfect smoke ring in Hamish's direction.

"Anything that happened on the night of the murder is relevant," said Hamish. "Either tell me here or come to the station with me and make a statement."

There was a long silence. Then Mr. Ferrari said, "I have come to love this village. I am part of it. I am involved in the welfare of Lochdubh. Sean Gourlay in the eyes of the villagers had outstayed his welcome. It was evident to all that he was the reason for Mrs. Wellington's distress, although no one knew why. I took it upon myself to tell him to move on."

"With threats?"

"Dinnae be daft," he said, his accent broadening. "I told him if he stayed on I would see to it that the shops did not serve him."

"And what did he say to that?"

"He said he would move."

Hamish leaned back in his chair and momentarily closed his eyes. He was in no doubt that Mr. Ferrari had threatened Sean with physical violence. Perhaps he had carried out that threat.

"I will type up a statement," said Hamish, "and get

you to sign it. I will also have to take statements from Luigi and Giovanni."

Mr. Ferrari carefully stubbed out his cheroot. He looked thoughtfully at Hamish from under heavy-lidded eyes. "I am not pleased that you are pursuing inquiries into the death of a piece of shit," he said evenly. "I am not pleased with you at all, Sergeant."

"Listen to me, Mr. Ferrari," said Hamish, standing up, "this is not Italy. There are no headmen in this village, and I for one will not tolerate anyone who tries to achieve his ends with threats. You are not pleased with me! Just who the hell do you think you are?"

Hamish stalked back to the station and typed up the statement. He took it back and waited until Mr. Ferrari signed it and then took statements from Luigi and Giovanni.

At five o'clock, Luigi and Giovanni called at the police station. With many smiles and deprecatory waves of the hands they said they had come to collect Mr. Ferrari's television set, which had been "on loan."

"You must hae done something to make them mad," said Willie after they had left, carrying the set between them. "Och, jist when I thought I might have a chance wi' Lucia."

"You've got a snowball's chance in hell," said Hamish with true Highland malice. "The only thing that's likely to marry you, Willie Lamont, is a vacuum cleaner."

"Fat lot you know, *sir*," said Willie. "Thon Lucia's a

real woman." And he wrenched off his apron, dragged on his coat and went out and slammed the door.

Hamish slumped down in his favourite armchair, tossed his cap on the floor and stretched out his long legs. He thought of the Curries, of Angela Brodie, of Mrs. Wellington and groaned. "Damn all women," he said and closed his eyes and fell fast asleep.

He plunged straight into a dream in which he had just got married to Priscilla and they were on their honeymoon. They were in a hotel bedroom and Priscilla was undressing and he was staring in horror at her flat, muscled, hairy chest. "What's the matter, Hamish?" laughed Priscilla. "Didn't you know I was a man?"

He woke up sweating and stared sightlessly across the room, his heart pounding. What a nightmare! It must have been because of the awful day and because of that transvestite he had seen on television.

And then he sat up straight. When he had woken Cheryl yesterday morning, she had been groggy with sleep and she had been wearing a dirty old night-gown. How could she have fled from him on a scooter one minute and been in bed the next? The route the figure on the scooter had taken through the trees had been *away* from the direction of the campsite.

He dived through to the office and phoned Strathbane and asked to speak to Jimmy Anderson. "Whit now?" demanded Jimmy.

"Look," said Hamish, "this may be a daft question, but among the so-called pop singers in Strathbane, is there one who dresses as a woman?"

"A transvestite like?"

"Aye, wi' orange hair, slim, maybe girlish-looking."

"There's the one wi' black hair, or had the last time I saw him."

"Name?"

"Real name I dinnae ken, for he hisnae been in trouble with us. Time was when we could hae banged him up for dressing like a lassie, but them were the good auld days."

"Name?" shouted Hamish.

"Bert Luscious, would you believe."

"Where...where does he live?"

"I don't know. But he does a turn at a drag club doon by the docks called Jessie's."

"A drag club in *Strathbane*!"

"We move wi' the times, Hamish, laddie, we move wi' the times. Started up a few months ago. Put a plain-clothes man in for a few nights, but he said it was all quiet, no drugs, no mayhem, jist a lot of fellows in lassies' frocks."

"Thanks," said Hamish feverishly.

"Whit fur? Are ye intae the marabou and rhine-stones yourself?"

"Maybe," said Hamish and put down the phone. He scrabbled in his desk and came up with a notebook he had used when Sean and Cheryl had appeared on that scooter. He had taken the number. But if she had sold it, he could not find out the new owner until morning. Damn. He should have phoned immediately after he got back.

He went to the Napoli restaurant. Willie was sitting comfortably at a corner table being waited on by Lucia. "I'm off again," said Hamish curtly. "You'd best get back to the station in case any urgent calls come through."

Lucia looked at Hamish as if he were a monster. Then, "Go along," she said quietly to Willie. "Giovanni will bring your meal and your wine over to you."

As Hamish left, Mr. Ferrari held open the door for him. His thin purplish lips were parted in a smile which did not reach his eyes.

Chapter Nine

When gloamin' treads the heels o' day,
And birds sit courin' on the spray,
Alang the flower'y hedge I stray,
To meet my ain dear somebody.

—Robert Tannahill

Hamish took Towser with him, frightened that a love-lorn Willie would neglect the dog. He put the dog's blanket and water bowl in the back of the Land Rover, along with a helping of cold pasta he had found in the kitchen.

As he once more took the long road to Strathbane, he wondered that a drag club could survive anywhere in the Highlands. "Jessie" was the Scottish word for an effeminate man, a shortened version of the old English sneer of jessamy. No doubt that was why the place was called Jessie's. He did not want to advertise to the customers that he was a policeman, but neither did he want to borrow a frock from Priscilla and dress up. He was not in uniform but in a dark-blue sweater, checked shirt and dark-blue cords. He could only hope that some of the other customers were similarly attired.

He found Jessie's on the waterfront in Strathbane, housed in what used to be a ship's chandler's. Music was thudding out into the acrid air of Strathbane. He locked the Land Rover after filling Towser's water and food bowls and made his way inside, blinking to accustom his eyes to the darkness.

To his relief, the customers were practically all in conventional dress and included some obviously staid married couples who had simply come to see the show. In order to get in, he had had to pay the club membership of five pounds. He was ushered to a table in a corner by a young man dressed unimaginatively in striped T-shirt and skin-tight black trousers who served him orange juice and charged him two pounds for it.

On the stage someone in low-cut gown and sequins and feathered headdress was belting out "Hello, Dolly." He was obviously the star turn, looking like a glamorous woman compared to the sequinned chorus who looked what they probably were, small Scotsmen with bad legs. As the show went on, Hamish was able to understand the club's obvious popularity with a respectable section of the population because it mostly consisted of popular numbers from musicals, all quite well staged and mostly well sung. But there was no sign of Bert Luscious.

He signalled to the waiter, told him he was a police-man, and asked to see the owner. After about fifteen minutes, the waiter returned and asked Hamish to follow him to "the back o' the house."

He pushed open a door and said, "Jessie'll see you now," and Hamish went in.

Jessie turned out to be the man who had sung "Hello, Dolly." He was still in costume but had removed his blond wig to reveal a shaven head. The small room was made up like a star's dressing-room in miniature with lights around the mirror and a Victorian chaise longue in one corner.

"What iss up?" demanded Jessie in an accent that Hamish guessed probably hailed from South Uist in the Outer Hebrides, having a soft, whistling sort of sibilancy.

"Nothing up with the club," said Hamish. "I'm looking for someone called Bert Luscious."

"Not on tonight, precious."

"Can you give me his address?"

"And why should I be doing that, officer?"

"Because I am on a murder inquiry and it is your duty to help the police."

Jessie sighed and then pulled a large book towards him, scattering sticks of grease-paint as he did so. With one large white well-shaped hand, he flicked through the pages. "Aye, here we are. Quite close by, he is. Number 141, Highland Towers, on the estate up back."

"Thanks," said Hamish.

Jessie batted his false eyelashes at him. "Enjoy the show, sweetie?"

"Yes," said Hamish awkwardly, backing towards the door. "Why Jessie?" he asked.

"Because that's what all those nasty little boys at school used to call me—Big Jessie. My real name is Cyril Crumb, and believe me, anything iss better than that."

As Hamish drove towards the tower blocks which overlooked the waterfront, he reflected dismally that he could hardly claim this night's expenses, as he was not even supposed to be in Strathbane.

Bert Luscious's flat was on the sixth floor but the urine-stinking lift was out of order and so he had to trudge up the stairs and then along a gallery which led outside the flats, listening to the sounds of drunken quarrels, crying babies and television sets coming through the thin walls.

Number 141 was in darkness but he could hear the blast of a stereo coming from inside, thumping out rap. He rang the bell. No answer. He thudded on the door and waited but no one came to answer it. He tried the handle and the door swung open.

A fetid, sweet smell met his nostrils and he groped about the minuscule hallway until he found the light switch. A joss-stick was burning in a milk bottle on a table, hence the smell. The noise of music was coming from behind a door to his right. He opened it.

He found himself looking into a living-room, cluttered and messy with dirty clothes strewn about the battered furniture. On a sideboard a large ghettoblaster shattered the air with sound. He crossed the room and switched it off.

Next door a television set mumbled on through the walls, punctuated with an occasional burst of canned laughter. "Anybody home?" he called.

He walked back into the hallway and tried the door opposite. This proved to be a squalid bedroom: unmade bed, dirty stained sheets, posters on the walls of singers with guitars.

He left that and tried the bathroom and then walked into a small kitchen at the back of the hall.

Bert Luscious was seated at the kitchen table, his long orange hair spilling out over a cheap plastic top. Hamish tried to rouse him and then saw the syringe lying beside his head, half covered by his hair. He felt his limp wrist. There was only a flutter of a pulse.

Hamish swore under his breath. It looked as if Bert had taken an overdose. He, Hamish, would have to explain his presence in Strathbane, for he would need to get Bert to the nearest hospital.

He found a telephone buried under a pile of clothes on the living-room floor and phoned for an ambulance, and then with great reluctance phoned Strathbane Police Headquarters. He asked to be put through to Jimmy Anderson, briefly told him what he had found and said he hoped it could somehow be kept from Blair at the moment.

"Everything can be kept from Blair at the moment," said Anderson cheerfully. "He's in the hospital wi' cirrhosis o' the liver. Be round right away."

Hamish began to search feverishly after drawing on a thin pair of gloves which he always kept on him for examining clues without leaving his own fingerprints on them. He found the papers which showed that Bert was now the owner of Cheryl's scooter. He found some photographs of Bert in action and was startled at the young man's resemblance to Cheryl.

Then, feeling like a criminal, he carefully put everything back where he had found it, knowing full well that he was not supposed to touch anything before the CID arrived. He had just finished when he heard the approaching wail of the ambulance and police cars.

Hamish explained to Jimmy Anderson that he had just heard that Bert had orange hair and performed as a woman and had wondered whether that might have been the way Cheryl could have been at Lochdubh murdering Sean when she was supposed to be on stage. But he said nothing of his find of the money and drugs, nor of the blackmailing of the women. For a mad idea had taken root in his brain, an idea that might flush out the murderer with the least scandal possible.

But he patiently went back to headquarters with Anderson and typed up a statement. The report from the hospital said Bert was in a very bad way and no one would be able to interview him for some time.

Hamish then drove out to Mullen's Roadhouse. Sure enough, Johnny Rankin and the Stotters were gyrating and howling to the end of their performance. Cheryl gave him a filthy look as she finally climbed down from the stage.

"Don't worry," said Hamish. "I'm not here to ask you any more questions. Did you collect all your belongings from the bus?"

"Yes."

"Well, I'm glad of that, for Sean's mother is coming up the day after tomorrow to take away her son's things. But before she touches anything, the forensic team is coming back because I have found some items for them that they missed before and that I am sure will give us definite proof of the murderer. I swear they're covered in fingerprints."

Cheryl shrugged and her hair fell forward to hide her face. "When's this forensic lot coming?" she asked.

"Let me see, this is Wednesday...no, it's Thursday already, so that means Friday morning I'm expecting them."

"Oh, aye." Cheryl turned away, indifference in every line of her body.

But it must work. It's got to work, thought Hamish as he drove home. I'll tell the Wellingtons, the Curries, and Angela Brodie, and Mr. Ferrari, too, that I've found stuff which will enable the forensic department to find the murderer. Forensic investigation is the new witchcraft. Any guilty person's going to be frightened of being smelt out.

And if it doesn't work, reflected Hamish sadly, I'll turn everything over to Strathbane and throw myself on Jimmy Anderson's mercy. What a gamble! What a thin chance! But the murderer, or murderess, must be badly frightened, must still be desperate to cover his or her tracks. And if I get whoever did it, then I have to gamble on that person keeping quiet about the blackmailing. If it's Cheryl, point out that she'll get a more lenient sentence; if it's Ferrari, he didn't know about the blackmailing anyway. But if it's one of the others, the blackmailing is their best excuse for the murder and whoever it is will damn the other two innocent blackmail victims when presenting her defence. But it can't go on. I'll have to try.

The next day, he decided that there must have been something in the orange juice he had bought at the club. He was behaving ridiculously. Better to wait until Bert recovered from his drug overdose and get Jimmy Anderson to find out if he had stood in for Cheryl on the night of the murder. Then question Johnny Rankin and the rest. Then see if Cheryl could be broken. It was possible she did not know of the blackmailing, but how could she not know? But something drove him on to get Mrs. Wellington, Jessie Currie and Angela Brodie on their own and tell them a variety of what he had told Cheryl. All looked at him hopelessly, as if they were exhausted with weeping and worry.

When Hamish returned to the police station, Willie said, "Jimmy Anderson was on the phone. You're to call right back."

Hamish phoned Strathbane and was put through to the detective. "It's Bert Luscious, real name Bert Maxwell," said Anderson. "He's been and gone and died on us. I had a go at Johnny Rankin and the rest and they swear blind Cheryl was with them all the time and I cannae break their story. Rankin's got enough syringe marks on his arms tae make him look like a walking pincushion, but he started screaming about police harassment and said he's been clean for months. We searched his flat and the others but couldnae find any drugs. Look, Hamish, Mullen tells me you've been tae the roadhouse and it's no' on your beat. You're going tae have to look the facts in the face, and it's that one o' that lot in Brigadoon up there did it, and stop running yourself ragged wi' a bunch o' daft men in women's frocks and a lot o' drug addicts who can't sing for twopence. Are you keeping anything back?"

Hamish said reluctantly, "I've got new evidence. Mrs. Wellington, the minister's wife, was back at the bus on the night of the murder, so was her husband, and so was the restaurant owner, Ferrari, and a couple of his relatives."

"And why havenae we seen those statements?"

"I've just done them," said Hamish.

"Look here, when is that mother coming up tae sell the bus?"

"In a few days' time."

"Well, I'm coming up there tomorrow to go over the whole thing again, and do you know why, Hamish Macbeth?"

"No."

"Because I've got a feeling in ma bones you're protecting someone. If Blair's as bad as I think he is, he'll have to retire and I'm in line for promotion, so it's no more easygoing auld Jimmy Anderson. See you in the morn."

Priscilla, thought Hamish. I need Priscilla, and as if on cue, Priscilla walked into the office.

"Sit down," said Hamish. "I'm in a grand old mess."

Willie came in with a tray of coffee. "Willie, could you take off your pinny and go on your beat," said Hamish. "We want to be alone."

"Why?"

"Use your brains, man, I've got something serious to ask Miss Halburton-Smythe."

"Oh, I see," said Willie. "I'll give you a long time then."

When Willie had gone, Hamish outlined what

had happened to date and his plans for catching the murderer.

"It might just work," said Priscilla. "What will you do if no one turns up?"

"I'll chust haff to tell Anderson everything."

"I suppose you can lie and tell him you just found the stuff. When do you expect your murderer to show?"

"After dark."

"That'll be about midnight, and even then it never gets really dark at this time of year," pointed out Priscilla. "If I were you, I would begin watching about ten. I've got a nifty little tape recorder up at the castle. I'll bring that and keep you company."

"Nice of you, but why?"

"Better to have proof and a witness."

"And what do I tell Willie?" asked Hamish.

"Tell him we're walking out. He thinks you're proposing to me anyway."

"Och, no," said Hamish. "The man can't be that daft."

"I'm telling you for a fact," said P.C. Willie Lamont in Patel's grocery store, "that Hamish Macbeth is in that polis station right now proposing marriage to Priscilla Halburton-Smythe."

"High time," said Mrs. Maclean.

"Our Hamish getting married!" Mr. Patel's dark

face lit up. He enjoyed a good bit of gossip. "Well, I never thought to see the day. My, my, my. And it's yourself, Mrs. Anderson, and how are you this fine day? Have you heard the news about our Hamish?"

A reporter from the *Strathbane and Highland Gazette*, who was standing patiently behind Mrs. Anderson waiting to buy a packet of cigarettes, pricked up his ears. Nice gossip piece. Forget the cigarettes. He'd better phone it over right away.

Hamish and Priscilla made their way to the field behind the manse by a circuitous route so that they would not be seen. This involved walking all the way over to Gunn's farm and then doubling back over the fields, past the greenish water-filled quarry and then up the steep path by the side of a cliff which overlooked the water, and so down towards the manse.

The twilight, or gloaming, as it is called in Scotland, was soft and clear. The residents of Lochdubh went early to bed, and as Hamish and Priscilla sat down in the field behind the shelter of the bus, the lights in the village were going out one by one.

They sat talking quietly of this and that but gradually fell silent, straining their ears for the slightest sound.

By one o'clock, the wind of Sutherland had risen and was moaning through the long grass and gaining in force every minute, filling the night with movement.

"We'll never hear anything in this," whispered Priscilla.

"I'm a fool," muttered Hamish bitterly. "These damn women should never have put themselves in a position to be blackmailed anyway, and they'd better face up and take their medicine. Why should I protect them and risk letting a murderer go free?"

"Because Sean was a worthless man and these women are not worthless. They just did not have any experience of evil before. They were all so innocent and he took advantage of that."

"Aye, I've had bad dreams over this. I had one about you, Priscilla."

"Oh, what was I doing?"

"We were on our honeymoon and you were taking off your clothes and you had a flat hairy chest."

"You know how to flatter a girl and make her feel good, Hamish."

"It wass chust a dream! You do not haff the flat hairy chest!"

"How do you know?" said Priscilla huffily.

"Because..." He grabbed her by the arms in a fierce grip. "Listen!" he muttered.

"Only the wind," whispered Priscilla.

"I don't *hear* anything exactly. I feel something coming."

" 'By the pricking of my thumbs, something wicked this way...' "

"Shhh!" He put a hand over her mouth.

Priscilla eased away from him and brought out the little tape recorder, switched it on and handed it to him.

Hamish stiffened like a hunting dog. His whole attention was focused on the packing case, whose light-brown sides glimmered faintly in the half-dark.

Then he let out a long "aaaah" of satisfaction.

"Stay here," he whispered. He walked slowly to where the bent figure was tearing the rocks out of the packing case.

"Cheryl Higgins," he said. "I charge you with the murder of Sean Gourlay." He shone a powerful torch full in her face.

"You're daft," she snarled. "Sean was hiding something here and he'd taken some o' ma things, and I remembered he might hae put them here."

So, thought Hamish bleakly, she could well stick to that story and look horrified and surprised when the contents of that bag were revealed.

He looked at her in sudden hatred and the lie sprang easily to his lips. "It won't do, Cheryl," he said. "Bert Luscious spoke before he died. He said he'd stood in for you on the night of the murder." And with the inspiration of the desperate, Hamish added, "and you promised him that scooter of yours if he did it."

She backed away from him, a slight figure in black leather, her long hair whipped this way and that by the wind. "You'll never get me in prison," she said viciously. "Not for that bastard. I told Sean I wus pregnant and he said, 'Here's money. Get rid of it.' I kep' the money and got it done on the National Health. Bastard."

"So you killed him," said Hamish.

"I didnae mean tae," she said, sounding suddenly weary. "I came back to see him. Johnny and the others said they would keep quiet. Sean loved me once. I drove the scooter from Strathbane and left it up on the moors and crept down into the village. There were some men at the bus and I waited, lying in the grass until they went away. Then I went in. Sean had got the sledge-hammer because he said there was a gale blowing up and he was going tae put ropes ower the bus. I picked up the sledge. 'Going to help me?' he said with that laugh, the way he had laughed when he told me tae get rid of the baby. Oh, God, he'd said he loved me and would always look after me." Her voice broke on a sob. "So I smashed him and smashed him until there was nothing left that would attract a woman again."

"What is here," asked Hamish, "that would incriminate you and not in the bus?"

"You didnae know," she marvelled. "You set me up and I fell for it. I hid the money and drugs for him and my fingerprints are all ower the stuff. And you didnae know. You're a bastard! I thought once you got my fingerprints on the stuff, you'd never leave me be. And I wanted the money and I wanted that video from the bus he was blackmailing those village women with. I was going to make them suffer."

Hamish stepped forward. "If you will accompany me to the police station, I—"

"NO!" she howled, a great scream which rose above the wind.

She whipped around and set out over the field like a deer. Hamish sprinted after her, caught his foot in a rabbit hole and went sprawling. Cursing, he got to his feet and ran on, deaf to Priscilla's cries behind him. The moon had risen and he could make out Cheryl's slight figure as it flew across the fields towards the quarry. As he pounded after her, he suddenly wondered if she knew about the quarry—she had always gone for walks around the village—and stopped, cupped his hands to his mouth and shouted a warning.

But she went straight on, straight to the edge and straight over.

Panting, he ran up and knelt down at the edge of the cliff over the quarry. The moon was shining on the spreading ripples on the water.

He hurtled down the bank at the side to where the waters of the old quarry were on a level with the ground, kicked off his shoes, laid the tape recorder on the shore and waded in. He dived and dived, groping desperately among the tentacles of the slimy weed which covered the bottom. From above the quarry came the sounds of voices.

He was nearing the end of his strength when his

searching hands located a body tied tightly in the embrace of the weed. He surfaced, gulped air and dived once more, this time with his clasp-knife in his hand. He cut the body free and dragged it to the surface.

A little group of villagers, who had been alerted by Priscilla's cries for help, stood silently huddled together on the beach. He laid Cheryl down. Dr. Brodie came hurrying up as Hamish was trying to revive the girl and pushed him aside. He felt Cheryl's pulse and then slowly shook his head.

"She's dead, Hamish. Nothing can be done for her now."

Ian Gunn, the farmer, drove up in his old rusty Land Rover. Cheryl's body was lifted into the back and the doors slammed on it. "Take it to the surgery and the ambulance from Strathbane will collect it," said Dr. Brodie. Ian nodded, climbed into the driving seat and drove slowly off, but the field was bumpy and he hit a rock and Cheryl's body jerked up in the back of the Land Rover, and for one horrible moment her white face, lit up by the moonlight, stared back at the watchers through the back windows.

Hamish gave a shiver. "We should have closed her eyes," he said wearily. "Why did we forget to close her eyes?"

Dawn was breaking. Hamish had changed into dry clothes. Detectives Jimmy Anderson and Harry MacNab were sitting in his living-room facing him. Priscilla sat beside Hamish on the sofa. In his bedroom, Willie slept on, as he had slept during the whole business.

"So, Hamish," said Anderson, "you've got it sewn up nicely. And you've got her confession on tape! Good man. Where is it?"

"It iss where I left it," said Hamish slowly. "It iss by the old quarry."

"No, it's not," said Priscilla cheerfully. "I picked it up." She opened her handbag and drew out the tape recorder.

Hamish gave her an agonized look. On that tape was Cheryl's voice not only admitting to the murder but talking about the drugs and money and the video. "Chust leave it be, Priscilla," he said quickly. "I'll type it up, Jimmy, and let you have it."

"No, let's hear it now," said Anderson. "How does it work? I was never any good wi' gadgets."

"Simple," said Priscilla, seemingly oblivious to Hamish's warning look. "You just press this button here."

Hamish covered his face with his hands as Cheryl's voice sounded into the room. The tape ran on to the bit about Cheryl confessing to smashing Sean and then there was Hamish's voice saying she should accompany him to the police station and Cheryl shouting "No!" and then nothing but the sound of Hamish running and panting and then his shouting a warning about the quarry.

Hamish slowly took his hands down from his face. Priscilla was sitting there calmly, as cool as a lettuce in a tailored green dress. The whole piece about the drugs, the money and the video had miraculously disappeared from the tape.

"Well, I must say you did a grand job, Sergeant," said Anderson. Hamish glanced at him. Could it be his imagination, or had Anderson become more pompous in manner and heavier in figure? Was the mantle of the repulsive Blair about to fall on his shoulders? "Of course," went on Anderson, "I consider it my duty to put in my report that the case could've maybe been solved earlier if you had not decided to investigate the Strathbane end on your own."

"That's unfair," said Priscilla.

"A good detective is always honest in his report," said Anderson.

The telephone rang in the police station and Hamish went through to answer it.

"When I'm Detective Chief Inspector, MacNab," said Anderson, "I'll be keeping Macbeth up to the mark. So he tricked that girl into a confession, but it's most irregular."

Hamish came in with a smile on his face. "I've got the grand news," he said. "That was Turnbull from Strathbane. He forgot to tell you last night that Blair is recovering. He'll soon be back on the job."

Anderson seemed to dwindle in size to his former

thin shape. "Pillock!" he said. "Here, Hamish, hae you any whisky?"

"A good copper does not drink on duty," said Hamish primly.

"Come on, Hamish, I'm off duty as from now."

"Particularly," went on Hamish, "a good copper who plans to put in a bad report about me."

"Did I say that?" Anderson looked wounded. "There'll be nothing but praise."

"In that case," said Hamish, "I seem to mind I have the bottle somewhere."

Chapter Ten

'Mid pleasures and palaces though we may roam,
Be it ever so humble, there's no place like home.

—John Howard Payne

Anderson and MacNab had finally left, Cheryl's body had been taken to Strathbane, and Hamish, supplied with black coffee by Priscilla, had typed up his report.

He came back into the living-room and sat down with a sigh. "What a night! Now, tell me how on earth you managed to doctor that tape."

"Easy. The minute I heard Cheryl was dead, I ran back to the castle with it. Someone had found it on the shore and I grabbed it and said I'd give it to you. I simply cut that bit out of the tape and then spliced it together again."

"How did you know how to do that?"

"Oh, some friend showed me how some time ago. You'd better get to bed, Hamish."

"Not yet. I've got to get that stuff up from under the packing case and I've got to erase the video. Are you awfully tired, or can you get the three women here?"

"Yes, but what about Willie?"

Willie was up and crashing dishes around in the kitchen to show his displeasure. He had learned of the solving of the murder from Priscilla as soon as he had got up and had come to the conclusion that Hamish had deliberately been keeping him out of the investigation.

Hamish went through to the kitchen. "Look, Willie," he said, "most of the investigations took place in Strathbane, where I shouldn't have been. I couldnae risk getting the both of us in trouble."

Willie was polishing dishes in the sink with a little mop. He hunched his shoulders and did not reply.

"It's no' as if you've shown any real interest in police work," said Hamish, exasperated.

"I would ha' shown interest enough with any encouragement," said Willie. "You wanted all the kludos for yourself."

"If you mean kudos, I did not. Take a walk, Willie. I really need to talk to Priscilla in private. Take the morning off." His voice grew wheedling. "Mr. Ferrari may not know the case is solved and he'd be right happy to hear about it."

"I suppose it's ma duty to tell him," said Willie reluctantly, "seeing as how the auld man said you were trying to pin the murder on him because he's a foreigner."

"Havers. But run along and tell him and don't come back until lunchtime."

Willie removed his apron. "I'll come back when I feel like it, *sir*."

When he had gone, Hamish returned to Priscilla and said, "That's got rid of him. Go and get the women here and I'll get that bag up from under the packing case."

Hamish went up to the field and looked about to make sure no one was watching before he took the rocks out of the packing case and shoved it aside. He took the metal box out of the bag and then replaced it with some of the rocks.

Mrs. Wellington, Jessie Currie and Angela Brodie were sitting in the living-room when he returned.

"Do the police know?" asked Mrs. Wellington, her face a muddy colour. "Miss Halburton-Smythe would not tell us anything."

"Only we know, us here in this room," said Hamish. He opened the box. "All the money Sean got from you will not be here, for I'm sure he spent a lot of it, but I'll leave it to you to divide up what's here, and Angela, you'd best put those packets of morphine back in the surgery."

The three women looked at him without moving. "Oh, the video," said Hamish. "Here it is." He put a couple of fire-lighters on the fire, lit them and then threw the video on top of them.

Priscilla slid quietly out of the room.

Jessie, Angela and Mrs. Wellington watched solemnly until the video disintegrated into a black molten mess.

"Now let's get to the money," said Mrs. Wellington with a return of her usual bossy manner.

Willie Lamont was met at the kitchen door by Lucia. She was carrying a sack of rubbish. "I'll take that," said Willie. "You should not be carrying heavy loads like that."

He walked round to the back of the restaurant and heaved the sack into the large rubbish container.

"You will make some lady a good husband, Weellie," teased Lucia.

He turned and looked at her. The wind of the night before had calmed down to a light breeze. Tendrils of hair were blowing about her pretty face. He heaved a great sigh.

"Hamish Macbeth has the right of it," he said sadly. "I'm an auld woman, always fussing ower the housework. What woman would want a man like that?"

Lucia looked at him, wide-eyed. "Do you mean, if you were married, you would *still* be doing the housework?"

"Aye, that's a fact, Lucia. I'd always be there, fussing and cleaning."

Her eyes began to glow. She thought back on her

young life in the village in Italy with her seven little brothers and sisters, a life of perpetual cleaning and drudgery. She raised her red hands and looked at them, turning them this way and that, and then she put them gently on Willie's shoulders.

"You have never tried to kiss me, Weellie."

He looked at her in surprise and then his eyes fell to that deliciously pouting mouth. He had dreamt of kissing Lucia, but always in some romantic setting, up on the heathery moors or out on a boat in the loch, but never had he imagined it as he was doing now, kissing her while the sea-gulls swooped and dived about the restaurant rubbish. He had never experienced anything like it. When he at last freed his mouth, he was trembling and tears were running down his cheeks.

"Don't make fun o' me," he said hoarsely.

"I'll never make fun of you," said Lucia, kissing the end of his pointed nose. "Not even after we're married."

"Married! You'd marry me? Oh, my heavens!"

"But you'd better go and see Mr. Ferrari and get his permission. Will we live in the police station?"

"Will we, hell!" cried Willie. "I've got a tidy bit put by and we'll get a nice house all to ourselves."

They went in to see Mr. Ferrari, who listened to them impassively and then said, "Lucia, there are vegetables to prepare in the kitchen."

Then he sat down at a restaurant table and waved a hand to indicate that Willie should sit opposite.

"Lucia is a good Catholic," began Mr. Ferrari.

"I'm a Roman Catholic myself," said Willie.

"But I haven't seen you at mass."

"A lapsed Catholic, but I can take it up agin," said Willie eagerly.

"And will you be able to support her on a policeman's pay?"

"Aye, I can that. I've got a good bit in the bank."

"How much?"

"About fifty thousand pounds."

"What! How did you get that?"

"I won one o' thae competitions in the newspapers."

Mr. Ferrari leaned back in his chair. "I hear the murder has been solved by Hamish."

"Aye," said Willie bitterly, "and he did his best tae keep me out of it. Wanted all the glory for hisself."

"Do you like police work?"

Willie looked puzzled. "I never really thought about it, to tell you the truth. Everyone says it's a good job and you get respect."

"But not from Hamish Macbeth. Would you expect Lucia to work once she was married?"

"Wouldn't dream of it," said Willie.

The lizard eyes looked at him with calculation. "You would be a boon to this restaurant of mine, Willie. Girls like Lucia I can get, but I am old and need someone to manage the place. Luigi and Giovanni would not mind. They are no good with orders and bookkeeping and know it. What would you say if I asked you to leave your job and come into business with me?"

Willie saw stretching out before him a life of endless cooking and cleaning and thought he might faint from excitement.

"Oh, that would be grand."

"Then I suggest you tell that lanky drip of nothing called Hamish Macbeth the good news as soon as possible. He has done better for himself than he deserves." Mr. Ferrari leaned over and picked up a copy of the local newspaper. "He is, I see, engaged to Priscilla Halburton-Smythe."

"Oh, aye," said Willie, "I knew that was on the cards."

Priscilla had arrived back at the police station with bottles of champagne which she had bought at Patel's. "I thought we would all celebrate the end of the nightmare," she said, popping a cork. "Hamish, are you sure you didn't slip about any of this to anyone other than us?"

"Of course not. Why?"

"Mr. Patel kept shaking my hand and saying, 'Congratulations.'"

He probably knows you were there with me when we caught Cheryl," said Hamish.

"That must be it," said Priscilla doubtfully.

Nessie Currie erupted into the room and glared at her sister. "So this is where ye are!" she cried. "And drinking champagne like the veriest whore. Shame on ye. Are ye not in enough trouble as it is? Are ye...?"

Jessie smiled mistily at her sister over the rim of her champagne glass as Mrs. Wellington interrupted Nessie's tirade with a booming cry of "Hamish has burnt the video and you've got most of your money back."

Nessie sank down slowly into a chair and heard the whole story. "Oh, my," she said weakly, "and here's me ranting and raving. And of course there's every reason why we should be drinking champagne on this happy day, Miss Halburton-Smythe. Yes, I'll hae a glass and drink to your health."

"Thank you," said Priscilla in surprise.

Angela smiled teasingly at Hamish. She already looked years younger. "John always said you'd never do it, Hamish, but I was sure you would."

"I'm surprised at Dr. Brodie," said Hamish. "I haff solved the murders afore."

"Oh, not *that*. When is it to be?"

"When's what?"

"Why, your wedding!"

"What wedding?" howled Hamish.

"It's in the *Gazette* this morning," said Angela, puzzled. "You and Priscilla."

"Oh, my poor father," said Priscilla weakly. "He'll have a stroke."

"You mean," said Angela, her face falling, "that you haven't...that you didn't know anything about it?"

"Not a thing."

The phone rang in the police-station office. Hamish went to answer it. It was Superintendent Peter Daviot from Strathbane. "Well done, Hamish," he cried.

"Thank you," said Hamish modestly. "I was just doing my job."

"Not your job, man, your engagement. Terrific news. My wife's going out to look for an engagement present for you."

"But—"

"Not another word, you sly dog!"

And the superintendent rang off.

"Don't worry, Hamish," came Priscilla's voice from next to him. "We'll get the paper to print an apology."

He twisted his head and looked up at her. She looked amused, cool and beautiful...and distant.

With one abrupt movement, he pushed back his chair, and reaching up an arm, jerked her down onto his knees and began to kiss her, dizzy with emotion, fatigue, whisky and champagne.

The phone began to ring again but both ignored it. Willie walked in and picked it up. "Oh, it's yerself, Mrs. Macbeth," he said to Hamish's mother. "Yes, that's right. Well, himself is tied up at the moment. I'll get him to ring back."

He shook his head over the entwined couple and went out.

"Who was that?" murmured Priscilla against Hamish's lips.

"Don't know and don't care. Kiss me again."

"Is this a proposal, Hamish?"

"Aye."

"Well, take your hand out of my brassiere and listen to me for a moment."

Hamish gave her a wounded look. "You're not going to be *sensible*, are you?"

"Yes, I am. I don't think I trust you, Hamish. I love you but I don't trust you. I think you've got too much of an eye for the ladies."

"But I'm proposing to *you*, Priscilla."

"Okay, but just an engagement, a *long* engagement."

"Anything you say."

"Do you love me?"

"I've been trying not to for years."

"Now kiss me again."

Willie arrived back at the police station. It was as quiet as the grave. He walked into the living-room and scowled at the mess of dirty glasses and empty champagne bottles. Then he saw a note addressed to himself pinned on Hamish's bedroom door. He took it down and opened it. It said, "Tell everyone I have gone out. Must get some sleep. Hamish."

But Willie wanted to tell Hamish that he was leaving, so he gently opened Hamish's bedroom door. Hamish and Priscilla were lying together on Hamish's narrow bed. They were both fast asleep. They were lying on top of the bedclothes, fully dressed with all their clothes, and with Towser at their feet, but Willie blushed furiously and quickly shut the door again.

Then he brightened as he turned and looked around the messy room. He would give the police station one last good clean-up.

Mr. Wellington returned home that evening after a round of visits to the old and sick in the parish. He expected his wife to be asleep. He had complained to Dr. Brodie about the number of sleeping pills she was taking, but Dr. Brodie said that she must be getting them from another doctor, possibly in Strathbane. To his surprise, he smelled cooking, delicious cooking. It seemed he had been having squalid cold meals for ages.

"Ah, there you are," said his wife briskly as he entered the large manse kitchen. "Sit down. Dinner's nearly ready. Steak-and-kidney pie, mashed potatoes and Brussels sprouts, and make sure you eat all your greens, dear. You've been looking peaky of late."

"Yes, my love," said the minister happily.

"Oh, by the way, that money that was missing from the Mothers' Union turned up again. It was left in the church hall on the kitchen counter…no note, no anything. We're all quite sure it was a passing tramp or someone like that who had a fit of conscience and put it back."

Mrs. Wellington briskly and efficiently took a golden-crusted steak-and-kidney pie out of the oven.

Mr. Wellington clasped his hands and bowed his head. "Thank you, God," he said.

"Why, you're praying," cried Mrs. Wellington.

"Why, so I am," said the minister.

Dr. Brodie could not quite put his finger on it but he knew that things had changed the minute he opened the door and walked into his house. He went into the kitchen. His wife was sitting behind a pile of textbooks as usual, but there seemed to be a lightness in the very air.

"I feel a bit daft," he said, sitting down. "I was checking the drugs cabinet and I found those missing packets of morphine. They'd got stuck inside a packet of something else. I should call Hamish."

Angela smiled at him. "Leave it till tomorrow. I thought we would eat out tonight. I've booked a table at the Napoli."

"Great idea. Why don't you wear one of your new dresses?"

"I haven't got them."

"What!"

"I sold them down in Inverness. That's where I've been today," lied Angela. "I got most of the money back."

"Well, good for you. I didn't know you could get any money at all for second-hand clothes."

"These were models."

"I don't know anything about women's clothes, but if it means dinner at the Napoli, then that's grand."

Hamish woke early in the evening and stretched out and felt around for Priscilla. But she had gone. He groaned and sat up and went through to the police office. There was a long string of messages and demands to call back. He began to work his way through them, starting with his mother, and so down to Jimmy Anderson.

"Thought you'd like to know," said Anderson, "that we got that pop band to crack and they admitted covering up for Cheryl."

"That's grand."

"The bad news is that I visited Blair in hospital. He's made a complete recovery, but he's been told to stay off the booze and go to Alcoholics Anonymous."

"God grant them the serenity when Blair turns up,

cursing and blinding, at one o' their meetings," said Hamish with feeling.

"Can you imagine what he'll be like sober?" demanded Anderson peevishly. "The only time that man's human is when he's drunk. Talking about getting drunk, are you celebrating your engagement?"

"I plan to. I've lost her for the moment."

"Good luck tae ye. Her father's probably taking a horsewhip to her right now. What d'ye think o' Willie leaving the force?"

"I didn't know. He didn't tell me."

"He's going into the restaurant business. The trouble is we cannae find a copper at the moment to replace him, so you're on your own again."

Bliss, thought Hamish, after he had rung off. Sheer bliss.

He picked up the phone again and rang the castle and with bad luck got Priscilla's father on the other end. In a mild voice, he asked to speak to Priscilla.

"Before I get my daughter," said the colonel in a low, quiet voice, quite unlike his usual blustering tones, "if you think you are going to marry her, you've got another think coming. She will never marry you, Hamish Macbeth, and I will do my best to stop you. I am warning you."

"So I'm warned," snapped Hamish. "Just get her."

When Priscilla answered, she said hurriedly, "Meet me at the Napoli in about ten minutes. I've got to get out of here."

"That bad?"

"Worse. He's gone all quiet and sinister and Mummy keeps crying and saying I'm ruining my life."

"They'll get used to it," said Hamish heartlessly.

The Napoli was crowded. Willie and Lucia were seated at the best table with Mr. Ferrari, all toasting each other with Asti Spumanti. Before Hamish could join Priscilla, Mr. Ferrari waved him over. "So what do you think about Willie managing this business for me?"

"Grand," said Hamish, shaking Willie's hand. "Just grand. All the best."

Mr. Ferrari gave him a baffled look. "You are pleased to be losing such a good officer?"

"I'm pleased because he's happy," said Hamish.

Mr. Ferrari gave a sudden amused shrug. "You are a man of many surprises, Hamish."

Hamish threaded his way through the tables towards Priscilla, accepting the congratulations of the locals.

She was wearing a slim low-cut silk dress with a delicate necklace of small emeralds set in gold. Her face was calm and beautiful.

He felt a momentary pang of unease. This was the beauty he was going to share his police-station life with! It seemed incredible.

"I know," said Priscilla sympathetically, although he had not spoken, "it takes some getting used to."

"It's been quite a day," said Hamish awkwardly. He felt desperately shy of her for the first time.

He fought to find a topic of conversation and then remembered that Sean's mother was due to arrive on the following day and that Ian Chisholm at the garage had promised to make her an offer for the bus. When he had exhausted that topic of conversation and ordered the meal, he sat in a miserable silence.

Priscilla stood up with one graceful fluid movement, came round the table and kissed him full on the mouth.

"Better?" she asked as she sat down again.

Hamish's face suddenly lit up with sheer happiness.

"Better? I'm in heaven!"

The next day dawned fine and warm. Hamish dealt with the painful business of Mrs. Gourlay, who turned out to be a small, quiet, faded lady, not in the least like her flamboyant son.

When it was all over, he went to the hen-house and dragged an old deck-chair out, cleaned it and put it on the patch of grass in front of the police station and stretched out on it.

"Quite like old times. I say quite like old times," came a familiar voice from the hedge.

Hamish straightened up and found the Currie sisters looking at him. But suddenly, as he looked at Jessie, he had an embarrassing picture of how she had looked naked on that video and somehow that picture seemed to have transferred itself in that moment from his mind to Jessie's.

She blushed deep red, gave a strangled squawk, and sped off, dragging her sister after her.

Hamish lay back in his deck-chair and grinned.

SAVOR THE FLAVORS

OF SCOTLAND—WITH ANOTHER

HAMISH MACBETH MYSTERY

BY M. C. BEATON!

Please turn the page
for a preview of

Death *of* Yesterday.

Chapter One

Send home my long stray'd eyes to me,
Which O! too long have dwelt on thee

—William Blake

Morag Merrilea was an art student, earning money in her summer holidays by working as a secretary for Shopmark Fashions in Cnothan in the Scottish county of Sutherland. She was English and considered herself a cut above her fellow workers. She was highly unpopular. Her appearance was unprepossessing. She had lank brown hair and rather prominent green eyes. But she had a passion for art and for studying faces.

Shopmark Fashions was a new factory on the outskirts of the village, risen out of an old derelict Victorian furniture store. Cnothan was a grim place with one main street running down to a man-made loch over which towered the grey walls of a hydro-electric dam.

Morag had taken the job because she had dreamt of a

romantic highland village, and had never quite got over
the culture shock of being in Cnothan where the sour
locals took pride in "keeping themselves to themselves."

She sat in her usual corner of the Highlander pub one
Saturday evening with her sketchbook, busily drawing the faces of people in the pub, and, also, the face of
someone looking in at the window. Morag always drank
alone. The other employees of the factory drank at a pub
down on the lochside and, strangely enough, Morag's
solitary drinking was not remarked on because of her
unpopularity and the locals shying away from any mention of her.

Although not particularly imaginative, she seemed
that particular evening to feel the remoteness, the very
foreignness of Sutherland pressing in on her, a claustrophobic sense that the great towering mountains were
creeping closer across the heathery moors. The result
was, she drank more than usual. The pub was quite full
with forestry workers, crofters, and the unemployed.
Morag was brilliant at drawing faces and felt the very
act of drawing people and putting them on paper put
them in her power.

At one point, she went to the lavatory. When she
returned, she found her sketchbook was missing. She
complained to the barman and to everyone around.
Getting nothing in reply but blank stares, she downed

her drink and made for the door. Morag collapsed outside and was taken to hospital.

After she came awake the following morning and received a lecture from a young doctor on the evils of drink, Morag was gripped with a sudden fear that she might be an alcoholic. She had drunk four pints of beer and assumed she had experienced a blackout. She could not remember yesterday evening at all.

She did have one friend at Hornsey Art College, where she had studied. She phoned her friend, Celia Hedron, and told her about losing her memory.

Celia said sharply, "Have you considered that someone might have slipped you a date rape drug? That blacks you out so you can't remember things."

This dramatic solution appealed to Morag, who did not like to think she was a common alcoholic. She dithered for a week before catching a bus from Cnothan and presenting herself at the police station in Lochdubh. She had been told that the police sergeant, Hamish Macbeth, was also responsible for policing Cnothan—along with vast tracts of Sutherland.

Her first impression of Hamish Macbeth was a bad one. When she arrived, he was upon a ladder clearing out the guttering. His lazy constable, Dick Fraser, a plump man with a grey moustache, was sleeping peacefully in the front garden on a deck chair.

"You!" shouted Morag. "Get down here immediately. I have a crime to report."

Hamish came slowly down the ladder. She saw a tall man with flaming red hair and hazel eyes.

"What seems to be the problem?" he asked.

Morag threw back her head and declared, "I have been drugged, raped, and my sketchbook has been stolen."

"Then you'd better come ben to the office," said Hamish mildly.

"Whassat?" mumbled Dick and went back to sleep.

Hamish led the way in at the side door, through the kitchen and into his small office, where he pulled out a chair for her. He wrote down the details of her addresses in Cnothan and London along with her phone numbers at home and work.

"It's like this," said Morag. She gave him her view of what had happened, along with details of her age, twenty-three, and her work as a secretary at the clothes factory.

"And when exactly did this take place?" asked Hamish.

"Last Saturday week."

Hamish had been taking notes. He put down his pen. "If you were drugged with some date rape drug, it would no longer be in your system. Were you checked for signs of rape?"

"Well, no."

"I think we should go to the hospital right away and have you checked."

Morag bit her lip. She had examined herself and knew there were no signs of bruising or forced entry. "I can't be bothered," she said.

"Then I don't see what you expect me to do," said Hamish patiently.

"You are a moron," said Morag. "You could at least make some push to get my sketchbook back—that is if you ever get off your arse and do anything."

"What were you sketching?"

"Faces of people in the pub. Oh, and someone who looked in at the window."

"Are you any good?" asked Hamish bluntly.

She opened her large handbag and pulled out a small sketchpad and handed it to him.

His interest quickened. She was very good indeed.

"I'll need to take a note of who was in the pub. Can you remember any names?"

"They're all just faces to me—Angus this and Jimmy that. I do not consort with the local peasantry. The factory staff drink at the Loaning down on the loch."

"With an attitude like that," said Hamish, the sudden sibilance of his accent showing he was annoyed, "I'm fair astounded that someone didnae try to bump you off instead of chust slipping something in your drink."

"You're as useless as the rest of . . ."

"Calm down, lassie. I hae this idea . . ."

"Wonders will never cease."

"Oh, shut up and listen for once in your life. I know a hypnotist down in Strathbane. He might be able to put you under and restore some o' your memory."

Morag's protruding eyes gleamed. The drama of such a suggestion appealed to her along with the idea of rattling the cage of whoever had drugged her drink.

"I'll make an appointment and let you know," said Hamish.

Hamish wondered as he set off for Strathbane later that day with Dick why he was even bothering to help such an unlovely character as Morag Merrilea. He cursed himself for not having asked exactly how much she had to drink. She could simply have had an alcoholic blackout.

Still, he reminded himself, he wasn't doing anything else at the moment. The summer was unusually warm with those nasty biting midges of the Highlands out in force. Patel's, the local shop in Lochdubh, had sold out of insect repellent.

As they mounted a crest of the road, Dick said, "Every time I see Strathbane, I'm right glad I'm out of it."

Strathbane was a blot on the beauty of Sutherland. Once a busy fishing port, it had died when the fishing stocks ran out. Drugs arrived, and it became a town with an air of dirt and desolation.

"I don't like this idea of a hypnotist," said Dick. "Sounds awfy like black magic."

"Och, even Strathbane police use Mr. Jeffreys from time to time."

"Did they say he would pay his bill?"

Hamish shifted uncomfortably in the driver's seat. He knew that Detective Chief Inspector Blair, the bane of his life, would have put a stop to it.

"It's fine," he said airily. "He'll just send in his bill as usual."

Dick was disappointed in Mr. Jeffreys. He had expected to meet an elderly guru.

But Jeffreys was only in his thirties, a thin man with brown hair in a ponytail, dressed in torn jeans and a T-shirt.

"Let me see," said Jeffreys. "I can fit her in at three o'clock next Saturday."

Hamish phoned Morag on her mobile. She was delighted. "Wait till those bastards in the pub hear about this!"

"I wouldnae go around shooting your mouth off," cautioned Hamish. "I'll collect you on Saturday and take you to Strathbane."

* * *

In the three days leading up to Saturday, Hamish and Dick pottered around the police station. To Dick Fraser, a portly man with a grey moustache, it was paradise. Viewed as useless by headquarters in Strathbane, he had been relocated to Lochdubh. He was a quiz addict, appearing on television quiz shows, and the kitchen in the police station gleamed with his winnings—an espresso coffee making machine, a dishwasher, a new washing machine, and a new microwave.

The single and widowed ladies of the village began to regard him as prime husband material, but Dick showed no interest, preferring to dream in a deck chair in the front garden by day and watch television in the evenings.

He was roused from his lethargy on Saturday by Hamish. "We'd better go and pick up yon Morag female," said Hamish. "Get your uniform on."

Morag rented a flat in a Victorian villa on the edge of Cnothan. When Hamish rang her doorbell, there was no reply. Morag's flat was on the top floor. He stood back and looked up. The curtains were open but there was no sign of anyone moving about.

"Silly cow," he muttered. "I'm sure she wouldnae have forgotten." He rang the landlady's bell.

Mrs. Douglas, the landlady, opened the door. She was a small round woman with thick glasses and an untidy thatch of grey hair.

"Whit now?" she demanded.

"We've come to collect Miss Merrilea," said Hamish patiently. "Is herself at home?"

"Dinnae ken."

"Would you please go and look?"

Grumbling, she shuffled off up the stairs. They waited in the warm sunlight.

At last she reappeared and handed Hamish a post-card. "This was stuck on her door," she said.

Typed neatly on a postcard was: "Gone to London. Will be in touch." It was not signed.

"I don't like this," said Hamish. "Would you mind showing us her flat?"

"Have ye a warrant?"

"No, I haff not!" said Hamish. "But if you don't let me in and show me her flat, I'll come back here with a warrant and I will turn this whole damn place upside down, including your premises."

"Here, now, no need for that," she said, thinking of the cash undeclared to the taxman hidden under her mattress. "I'll get the key."

They followed her into a shadowy hall lit with coloured harlequin diamonds of light from the sun shining through the stained-glass panel on the front door.

Dick eyed the steep stairs. "I'll be waiting for ye outside, sir," he said to Hamish.

"Oh, all right," said Hamish crossly.

He followed Mrs. Douglas as she panted up the

stairs. She inserted a key into a door on the top landing. "There's no need for you to wait," said Hamish. "I'll bring you down the key when I've finished."

The flat consisted on a small living room, a cell of a bedroom, a kitchen unit behind a curtain, and a shower. The living room contained a small card table laden with artist's materials and two hardback chairs by the window. There was a dingy print of *The Stag at Bay* over the empty fireplace. One battered armchair was beside the fireplace facing a small television set. Planks on bricks along one wall supplied bookshelves.

Hamish went into the bedroom. He opened the wardrobe. A few skirts and blouses hung there and a winter coat. On top of the wardrobe was a large suitcase. He hauled it down and opened it up. It was empty. He put it back and then opened a chest of drawers. There were various surprisingly saucy items of lingerie: thongs and stockings with lace tops.

He sat down on the bed and looked round. She might have had a backpack of some kind to take a few clothes with her. There was no sign of a handbag, passport, or wallet.

He locked up and went downstairs to where Mrs. Douglas was waiting in the hall. "Did she have a car?" he asked, handing over the keys.

"No, she had a bike."

"And where does she keep it?"

"Just outside. But it's no' there."

"When did you last see her?"

"Cannae bring tae mind."

"Think!"

"Oh, I mind now. It was yesterday morning. Herself was just off tae work."

"Was she carrying a suitcase or any sort of luggage?"

"No. She just got on her bike and went off, same as ever."

Hamish felt uneasy. He put the postcard in a forensic bag and went out to join Dick.

"We'd better check where she works," he said. "I've got a bad feeling about this."

At Shopmark Fashions, they found that Morag worked as secretary to the boss, Harry Gilchrist. Mr. Gilchrist kept them waiting ten minutes, which Hamish put down to the usual pompous Scottish boss's way of trying to seem important.

Mr. Gilchrist was a tall thin man in his forties. He had thick black hair in a widow's peak above a sallow face and wet brown eyes.

"Working on Saturday?" asked Hamish.

"Work never stops," said Gilchrist. "What do the police want with me?"

"Did Morag Merrilea turn up for work yesterday?"

"As a matter of fact, she didn't. I meant to send

someone to check on her on Monday if she was still absent."

"She left a postcard on the door of her flat saying she had gone to London."

"Isn't that just typical of staff these days!" raged Gilchrist. "Well, if you come across her, tell her she's fired."

"Did she say anything about going to see a hypnotist?"

"No. A hypnotist? Why?"

Hamish explained about the suspected drugged drink and the missing sketchbook.

"Oh, that? She was complaining about that all over the place. She did drink a fair bit. She was in the habit of making things up."

"Is there anyone she was close to?"

"She kept herself to herself."

Like the whole of bloody Cnothan, thought Hamish.

Dick and Hamish next went to the Highlander pub. Pubs all over Britain had been smartened up with restaurants and pleasant décor, but the Highlander had been unmoved by time. There was one dim room with scarred tables and rickety chairs. The walls were still brown with nicotine from the days before the smoking ban. The only food on offer was in a glass case on the counter: tired-looking sandwiches and a solitary mutton pie.

Hamish recognised the barman and owner, Stolly Maguire. Stolly was polishing a glass with a dirty rag when they approached him. He was a thickset man with a bald head with a tank top strained over a beer belly.

Hamish explained they were trying to find out the whereabouts of Morag Merrilea.

"Thon artist?" said Solly. "Havenae seen her. Usually comes in Saturday evening."

"Two Saturdays ago," said Hamish patiently, "did you notice anyone approaching her table when she went to the toilet?"

"Naw. It was fair busy."

Hamish turned round and surveyed the customers, a mixture of crofters, shepherds, builders, and the unemployed.

"Which one of them was here two Saturdays ago?"

"I cannae mind," said Stolly. "Ask them? I saw her collapsing outside the door and phoned for an ambulance."

So Hamish and Dick went from table to table to receive surly answers to the effect that they had seen her on that Saturday but hadn't noticed anyone taking her sketchbook or putting something in her drink.

But a youth with greasy hair said he had noticed a stranger. "Can you describe him?" asked Hamish. "What is your name?"

"Fergus McQueen."

"Well, Fergus, what did he look like?"

"Hard tae tell. He had wan o' thae baseball caps pulled right down. Small and skinny."

"What was he wearing?"

"Black T-shirt, black jeans."

"The cap. Did it have a logo on it?"

"Naw. It was dark green with an orange stripe."

"Give me your address. We may want you to come to Strathbane and help a police artist make a sketch."

Back at Lochdubh, Hamish sat down at the computer in the police station office and sent over a report. He felt uneasy. It was too much of a coincidence that she should disappear when she had an appointment with the hypnotist.

To his amazement, he got a call from Detective Sergeant Jimmy Anderson later that day. "Blair's decided to look into it," he said.

"Why? I thought he'd delight in shooting the whole thing down," said Hamish.

"I think he feels if there is a crime, then he wants to be the one to solve it. You've stolen his glory too many times."

"I'd better get back to Cnothan and join him."

"He says you're to sit tight and look after your sheep and leave it to the experts."

Hamish groaned. He knew that Blair's blustering, bullying tactics would make the locals clam up even more.

  *   *   *

Hamish waited gloomily for the inevitable. Sure enough, it came later with an e-mail from Blair telling him it was a wild-goose chase and to stop wasting police time and, furthermore, never again try to employ the hypnotist without first getting clearance.

Undeterred, Hamish went back to Cnothan, knocking on doors, questioning one after the other without success.

He was furious when he returned to Lochdubh to receive a phone call from Superintendent Daviot. The locals in Cnothan had complained of police harassment. Blair had found nothing. Hamish was to leave it all alone.

The weather was unusually hot. Three weeks after the disappearance of Morag Merrilea, two men were loading bales of T-shirts onto a lorry outside Shopmark Fashions when they suddenly stopped their work.

"Thon's an awfy smell from that bail," said one, "and it's heavy, too."

"Better cut it open," said his companion. "There's maybe a dead animal inside."

They sliced the twine that held the bail and unrolled it.

The dead and decomposing body of Morag Merrilea rolled out and lay under the eye of the glaring sun.

SAVOR THE FLAVORS

OF SCOTLAND—WITH ANOTHER

HAMISH MACBETH MYSTERY

BY **M. C. BEATON!**

*Please turn the page
for a preview of*

Chapter One

See, the happy moron,
He doesn't give a damn,
I wish I were a moron,
My God! perhaps I am!
—Anonymous

Constable Hamish Macbeth sat in the small country bus that was bearing him away from Lochdubh—away from the west coast of Sutherland, away from his police-station home. His dog, Towser, a great yellowish mongrel, put a large paw on his knee, but the policeman did not notice. The dog sighed and heaved itself up onto the seat beside him and joined his master in staring out of the window.

The bus driver was new to the job. "Nae dugs on the seats," he growled over his shoulder, determined not to be intimidated by Hamish's uniform. But the constable gave him a look of such vacant stupidity that the driver, a Lowland Scot who considered all Highlanders inbred, decided it was useless to pursue the matter.

Misery *did* make Hamish Macbeth look dull-witted. It seemed as if only a short time ago he had been happy and comfortable in his own police station in Lochdubh, and then orders had come that he was to relieve Sergeant MacGregor at Cnothan, a crofting town in the centre of Sutherland. In vain had he invented a crime wave in Lochdubh. He was told that protecting the occasional battered wife and arresting a drunk once every two months did not amount to a crime wave. He was to lock up the police station and go by bus, for Sergeant MacGregor wished his stand-in to keep his car in running order.

Hamish hated change almost as much as he hated work. He had the tenancy of some croft land next to the police station at Lochdubh, where he kept a small herd of sheep, now being looked after by a neighbour. He earned quite good money on the side from his small farming, his poaching, and the prize money he won for hill running at the Highland Games in the summer. All that he could save went to his mother and father and brothers and sisters over in Cromarty. He did not anticipate any easy pickings in Cnothan.

Crofters, or hill farmers, always need another job because usually the croft or smallholding is too small a farm to supply a livelihood. So crofters are also postmen, forestry workers, shopkeepers, and, in the rare case of Hamish Macbeth, policemen.

It was the end of January, and the north of Scotland was still in the grip of almost perpetual night. The sun rose shortly after nine in the morning, where it sulked along the horizon for a few hours before disappearing around two in the afternoon. The fields were brown and scraggly, the heather moors, dismal rain-sodden wastes, and ghostly wreaths of mist hung on the sides of the tall mountains.

There were only a few passengers on the bus. The Currie sisters, Jessie and Nessie, two spinster residents of Lochdubh, were talking in high shrill voices. "Amn't I just telling you, Nessie?" came the voice of Jessie. "I went over to the Royal Society for the Prevention of Cruelty to Animals at Strathbane last week and I says to the mannie, 'I want a humane trap to catch the ferret that has been savaging our ducks.' He gives me the trap, and he says, 'You take this here humane trap, and you humanely catch your ferret, and then, if you want my advice, you will humanely club the wee bastard to death.' Sich a going-on! And him supposed to be against cruelty. I have written to our Member of Parliament to complain most strongly."

"You told me a hundred times," grumbled Nessie. "Maybe he was right. For all you caught in that humane trap was the minister's cat. Why don't you tell Mr. Macbeth about it?"

"Him!" screeched Jessie. "That constable is a poacher and it was probably his ferret."

The bus jerked to a halt and the sisters alighted, still quarrelling.

Three months in Cnothan, thought Hamish, absentmindedly scratching Towser behind the ears. They say Lochdubh is quiet, but nothing ever happens in Cnothan, and nothing ever will. Did I not have the two murders in Lochdubh?

He thought of the murder that had taken place last summer and how it appeared to have brought him closer to the love of his life, Priscilla Halburton-Smythe. But Priscilla, the daughter of a local landowner, had then left, just before Christmas, to go to London to find work. She never stayed away for very long. She might even be heading north now, and would return to Lochdubh to find him gone.

"And she will not be caring one little bit!" said Hamish suddenly and loudly. The bus driver bent over the wheel and congratulated himself on his decision to leave this crazy copper alone.

Hamish knew Cnothan and thought it must be the dullest place in the world. Although designated a town, it was about the size of a tiny English village. He remembered the inhabitants as being a close, secretive, religious bunch who considered anyone from outside an interloper.

At last, he was the only passenger left on the bus. The bus lurched and screeched around hairpin bends, finally racing out of the shadow of the tall pillared mountains to plunge down into the valley where Cnothan stood, in the middle of Sutherland.

Hamish climbed down stiffly and collected his belongings, which were packed into a haversack and an old leather suitcase. The bus departed with a roar and Hamish pushed his peaked hat back on his fiery hair and looked about him.

"High noon in Cnothan," he muttered.

It was the lunch-hour, which meant all the shops were closed and the main street was deserted. A savage wind screamed down it. Not even a piece of scrap-paper was borne on the wind. The town had a scrubbed, grey, antiseptic look.

Cnothan stood on the edge of an artificial loch caused by one of the ugliest hydroelectric dams Hamish had ever seen. What you saw was what you got. There were no quaint lanes or turnings. One straight main street led down to the loch. There were four grocer's shops, which all sold pretty much the same sort of goods, a hardware, a garage, a craft shop, a hotel, a fish-and-chip shop, a butcher's, a pub, and an enormous church. The government-subsidized housing was tucked away on the other side of the loch, segregated from Cnothan's privately owned houses, which were all very small and drab and looked remarkably like the government ones.

The town was so barren, so empty, it reminded Hamish of scenes in a science-fiction movie he had once seen.

And yet he was aware of eyes watching him, eyes hidden behind the neatly drawn lace curtains.

He opened the garden gate of the bungalow nearest him, called Green Pastures, and went up and rang the brass ship's bell that hung outside the door. Silence. A

plaster gnome stared at him from the garden and the
wind moaned drearily.

A mail-order magazine protruded from the garbage
bin beside the door. Hamish twisted his head and read
the name on it. Mrs. A. MacNeill. At last he heard footsteps approaching. The door was opened a few inches
on a chain and a woman's face peered through the
crack, one of those sallow Spanish types of faces you
find in the Highlands of Scotland.

"What is it?" she demanded.

Now Hamish knew in that instant that the woman
knew exactly who he was. Her manner was too calm.
For in a relatively crime-free area, the arrival of a policeman on the doorstep usually creates terror because it
means news of a death or accident.

"I am Constable Macbeth," said Hamish pleasantly,
"come to replace Mr. MacGregor who is going on holiday. Where is the police station?"

"I dinnae ken," said the woman. "Maybe it's up the
hill."

"At the top of the main street?" asked Hamish. He
knew the woman knew perfectly well where the police
station was, but Hamish was an incomer, and in
Cnothan, you never told incomers anything if you could
help it.

"It could be, but why don't you ask someone else?"
said the face at the door.

Hamish leaned against the door jamb and studied the
sky. "Aye, it iss blowing up," he said in his soft Highland voice, which became more sibilant when he was

angry or upset. "Now, Mr. MacGregor, he will be going to Florida to visit his brother, Roy. It will be hot there this time of year."

"Aye, it will," said the woman.

"And I call to mind he has the sister in Canada."

The chain dropped and the door opened another few inches. "That's Bessie," said the woman. "Her that is in Alberta."

"True, true," agreed Hamish. "And you are Mrs. MacNeill?"

"Now, how did you ken that?" asked Mrs. MacNeill, opening the door wide.

"Oh, hass not everyone heard of Mrs. MacNeill," said Hamish. "That's why I called. People are not often anxious to give directions, but I said to myself, that Mrs. MacNeill, being a cosmopolitan sort of lady, would help if she could."

Mrs. MacNeill simpered awfully. "You are asking about the police station. Yes, as I was saying, it is right at the top of the main street on the left. They are packed and ready to leave."

"Thank you." Hamish touched his cap and strolled off. "Cantankerous auld bitch," he muttered to Towser, "but there was no point in asking anyone else, for I suppose they'll all be the same."

At the top of the main street was a long, low, grey bungalow with the blue police lamp over an extension to the side. A small angry police sergeant was striding up and down outside.

"What kept ye?" he snapped. And then, before

Hamish could open his mouth, he went on, "Come in. Come in. But leave that dog outside. There's an old kennel at the back. It can sleep there. No dogs in the house."

Hamish told Towser to stay and followed the sergeant into the house. The sergeant led the way through to the extension. "Here's the desk, and don't you mess up my filing system. And there's the keys to the cell. You'll have trouble wi' Sandy Carmichael of a Saturday. Gets the horrors something dreadful."

"If a man has the DTs, isn't it better to get him to the hospital?" asked Hamish mildly.

"Waste o' public money. Jist strap him down on the bunk and let him rave away until morning. Come ben and meet the wife."

Hamish loped behind the bustling policeman. "She's in the lounge," said Sergeant MacGregor. Mrs. Mac-Gregor rose to meet them. She was a thin, wispy woman with pale eyes and enormous red hands. Hamish's pleasantries were cut short.

"I like to keep the place nice," said Mrs. MacGregor. "I don't want to come back from Florida and find the place like a tip."

Hamish stood with his cap under his arm, his hazel eyes growing blanker by the minute. The living-room in which he stood, which had been exalted to a lounge by the MacGregors, was a long, low room with pink ruched curtains at the windows. A salmon-coloured three-piece suite, which looked as if it had been delivered that day, stared back at him in all its nylon vel-

veteen overstuffedness. The walls were embellished
with highly coloured religious pictures. A blonde and
blue-eyed Jesus suffered the little children to come unto
him, all of them dressed in thirties school clothes and all
of them remarkably Anglo-Saxon–looking. A carpet of
one of the more violent Scottish tartans screamed from
the floor. There was a glass coffee-table on wrought-
iron legs in front of the sofa, and a glass-and-wrought-
iron bar stood in one corner, with glass shelves behind
it lit with pink fluorescent strip lighting and containing,
it seemed, every funny-looking bottle ever invented. An
electric heater with fake logs stood in the fireplace. In
the recesses of the room were glass shelves containing
a startling variety of china ornaments: acid-green jugs
in the shape of fish, little girls in pastel dresses holding
up their skirts, bowls of china fruit, dogs and cats with
Disney smiles on their highly glazed faces, and rows of
miniature spun-glass objects, of the type of spun glass
you see at fairgrounds. On a side table lay a large Victorian Bible, open at a page where there was a steel en-
graving of an epicene angel with scaly wings throwing
very small anguished people in loincloths down into a
fiery pit.

Mrs. MacGregor then led him from one frilly over-
furnished bedroom to another. The bungalow boasted
five.

"Where's the kitchen?" asked Hamish, finding his
voice.

She trotted on her high heels in front of him, head
down, as if charging. "In here," she said. Hamish stifled

a sigh of relief. The kitchen was functional and had every labour-saving device imaginable. The floor was tiled, and there was a good-sized table. He decided to shut off that terrible lounge for the duration of his stay.

"Have you got television?" he asked.

Mrs. MacGregor looked up at the tall, gangling policeman with the fiery-red hair and hazel eyes. "No, we don't believe in it," she said sharply, as if debating the existence of little green men on Mars.

"I see you have the central heating," remarked Hamish.

"Yes, but we have double glazing on the windows, so you'll find you hardly need it. It's on a timer. Two hours in the morning and two in the evening, and that's enough for anyone."

"Well, if I could chust haff a word with your good man . . ." began Hamish, looking around for the police sergeant, who had disappeared during the tour of the house.

"There's no time, no time," she said, seizing a bulging handbag from the kitchen counter. "Geordie's waiting with the taxi."

Hamish looked at her in amazement. He wanted to ask MacGregor about duties, about where the keys to the car were kept, about how far his beat extended, about the villains of the parish. But he was sure the MacGregors were cursed with what he had rapidly come to think of as Cnothanitis: Don't tell anyone anything.

He followed her out to the taxi. "So you'll be away

three months, then?" said Hamish, leaning on Mac-
Gregor's side of the taxi. The sergeant stared straight
ahead. "If you'd get out of the road, Constable," he said,
"we might be able to get to the train on time."

"Wait a bit," said Hamish. "Where are the keys to
your car?"

"In it," snapped MacGregor. He nodded to the
taxidriver and the cab moved off.

"Good riddance," grumbled Hamish. He jerked his
head to Towser, who followed him into the kitchen.
Hamish took the central heating off the timing regulator
and turned up the thermostat as high as it would go and
started to examine the contents of the kitchen cupboards
to see if there was any coffee. But the cupboards were
bare; not even a packet of salt.

"You know, Towser," said Hamish Macbeth, "I hope
they get hijacked to Cuba."

He went through to the office and examined the files
in a tall filing cabinet in the corner. It was full of sheep-
dip papers and little else. Not dipping one's sheep
seemed to be considered the major criminal offence in
Cnothan. There came a crashing and rattling from the
kitchen. He ran through. Towser had his large head in
one of the bottom cupboards, which Hamish had left
open, and was rummaging through the pots and pans.

"Get out of it, you daft animal," said Hamish. "I'll
just away to the shops and see if I can get us some
food." He searched until he found a bowl and filled it
with water for the dog. Then he ambled out of the house
and down the main street. The lunch-hour was over and

the shops were open again. People were standing in little knots, gossiping, and as he passed, they stopped talking and stared at him with curious and unfriendly eyes.

He bought two bags of groceries and then made his way down to the garage, which also sold household goods. He asked if he could rent a television set and was curtly told by a small man whose face was set in lines of perpetual outrage that no, he could not. To the shopkeeper's irritation, Hamish did not go away, but kept repeating his question in a half-witted sort of manner, looking around the other customers as he did so.

A small, thin, birdlike woman with sharp features came up to him. "You will be Mr. MacGregor's replacement," she said briskly. "I am Mrs. Struthers, the minister's wife. Can we expect to see you at church on Sunday?"

"Oh, yes," said Hamish amiably. "My name's Macbeth. I am a member of the Free Church myself." Hamish had taken careful note of the denomination of Cnothan's main church. He was not a member of the Free Church, or, indeed, of any other church.

"Well, that's splendid!" cried Mrs. Struthers. "Now, I heard you asking about a telly. We have a black-and-white one we are going to raffle at Easter. I could lend you that."

"Very kind of you," said Hamish, smiling down at her. That smile changed his whole face. It was a smile of singular sweetness.

In no time at all, Hamish was resting his boots on a

footstool in the manse and being plied with tea and scones.

"I am thinking, Mrs. Struthers," said Hamish, "that it will be a wee bit difficult for me here. They never did like incomers in Cnothan."

"Well . . ." said Mrs. Struthers cautiously, going to the window to make sure there was no sign of her husband returning from his rounds, her husband having preached about the iniquities of gossip the previous Sunday, "people here are very nice when you get to know them. All it takes is a few years."

"I haven't got the time," said Hamish. "I'm only here for three months."

"They'll come around quicker," she said, "because they're all united against a really nasty incomer." She looked around and her voice dropped to a whisper. "An Englishman."

"Oh dear," said Hamish encouragingly. "They do not like the English?"

"It's not that," said the minister's wife. "It's just he's such a know-all. It's a crofting community round here. They don't like being told how to run things, particularly by an outsider, but Mr. Mainwaring, that's his name, *will* tell them what they are doing wrong. Not in a nasty way, mind. But as if he's laughing at them. His poor wife. He won't even leave her to run the house, but supervises her cooking. He even *chooses her clothes* for her!"

"The fiend!" cried Hamish, registering extreme

shock, very gratifying to the minister's wife, who had not had such an appreciative audience in years.

"Have another scone, Constable. Yes, she is a member of the Women's Rural Institute and gave us a very good lecture on how to dry and arrange flowers. Most stimulating. She was doing very well, but he walked in at the question time and started grilling her—his own wife!"

"Fancy!"

"Yes. And she turned as red as fire and began to stammer. Wicked it was. And . . ."

The sound of a car crunching on the gravel outside made Mrs. Struthers turn as red as fire herself. "I had better go," said Hamish, not wishing to waste time talking to the minister.

But as he rose to his feet, Mr. Struthers, the minister, came in. He had a pale face and pale-blue eyes and a thin mouth. His tow-coloured hair was carefully sleeked down. Mrs. Struthers, rather flustered, made the introductions. "I trust you have not been gossiping," said the minister severely.

"On the contrary," said Hamish, "your good lady has just been encouraging me to visit the kirk on the Sabbath. She was telling me all about your powerful sermons."

He shook hands with the minister, collected the small television set, and said goodbye. The minister's wife went to the window and watched the tall figure of the constable as he walked away with a rather dreamy smile on her face. "Such a fine man," she murmured.

Hamish ambled up the main street, comfortably full

of tea and home-made scones and jam. At the top, opposite the police station, he noticed an old cottage, set a little back from the road, with a sign outside which said, PAINTINGS FOR SALE.

There was what appeared to be a teenage girl digging the garden. As if aware she was being watched, she turned around, saw Hamish, and came up to the garden gate. Her figure was as trim and youthful as a girl's, but Hamish judged her to be about the same age as himself—in her thirties. She had an elfin face, a wide smile, and a mop of black curls.

"Jenny Lovelace," she said, holding out a small, earthy hand.

"Hamish Macbeth," said Hamish, smiling down at her. "Is that an American accent?"

"No, Canadian."

"And what are you doing in the wilds of Sutherland, Miss Lovelace?" asked Hamish, putting down the television set and two grocery bags on the ground and shaking her hand before leaning comfortably on the gate.

"I wanted peace and quiet. I came over on a holiday and stayed. I've been here four years."

"And do you like it? I gather they don't like incomers here."

"Oh, I get along all right. I like being alone."

"I get the idea life has been easier for the incomers since a certain Mr. Mainwaring arrived. He sounds like a right pain in the neck."

Jenny's face hardened. "Mr. Mainwaring is about the

only civilized person in the whole of this place," she said sharply.

"I always go and put my big foot in it," said Hamish sadly. "It comes from not being in the way of talking to pretty girls. My mind gets all thumbs."

Jenny giggled. "Your mind doesn't have thumbs," she said. "Gracious! What's that terrible howling coming from the police station?"

"It's my dog, Towser. He wants his food, and when he wants his food, he screams for it. I'd best be on my way."

"Drop round for a coffee," said Jenny, turning away, as Hamish stooped to pick up his belongings.

"When?" Hamish called after her.

"Any time you like."

"I'll drop by the morn," called Hamish, feeling suddenly happy.

Towser's howling stopped when he saw his master. He lay on the kitchen floor and stared at Hamish with sorrowful eyes. "I've got some liver for ye," grumbled Hamish, pouring oil in a pan. "See, low-cholesterol oil, good for your fat heart." The doorbell on the police-station extension sounded shrilly. Hamish made a move to answer it. Towser started to howl again.

Hamish ran and wrenched open the door. A middle-aged man stood on the step. He was tall, well-built, and had a large round head and neat prim features, small round eyes, a button of a nose, and a small primped mouth. Although he must have been nearly sixty, he had a thick head of brown hair, worn long so that it curled

over his collar. He was wearing a waxed coat with a cor-
duroy collar, gabardine breeches, lovat stockings, and
brogues—and a red pullover. English, thought Hamish.
They aye love thae red pullovers.

"Come in and I'll be with you in a minute," gabbled
Hamish as Towser's howling rose to a crescendo. Hamish
darted back to the kitchen and put the liver in the frying
pan. When it was ready, he cut it up into small pieces,
arranged it on a dish, and put it in front of the dog.

"So we've lost one fool of a policeman to find another," said a sarcastic upper-class–accented voice from
the doorway of the kitchen. "Let me tell you, Constable,
that I am going to write to your superiors and say that
feeding good butcher's meat to a spoilt mongrel takes
precedence in what's left of your mind over solving
crime."

"Sit yerself down, Mr. Mainwaring," said Hamish,
"and I'll attend to you. I havenae had time to draw
breath since I arrived."

"How do you know my name?"

"Your reputation goes before you," said Hamish.
"Now, we can stand here exchanging insults or we can
get down to business. What's the crime?"

William Mainwaring drew out a kitchen chair and sat
down and looked up at the tall policeman. He took out
a pipe and lit it with precise, fussy movements. Hamish
waited patiently.

"You ask me what the crime is?" said Mainwaring finally. "Well, I'll tell you in one word:

"Witchcraft."

SAVOR THE FLAVORS

OF SCOTLAND—WITH ANOTHER

HAMISH MACBETH MYSTERY

BY **M. C. BEATON!**

Please turn the page
for a preview of

Death *of a* Kingfisher.

Chapter One

Where'er you walk cool gales shall fan the glade;
Trees, where you sit, shall crowd into a shade;
Where'er you tread, the blushing flow'rs shall rise,
And all things flourish where'er you turn your eyes.

—Alexander Pope

It is a well-known fact that just when a man reaches his early thirties and thinks he is past love, that is when love turns the corner and knocks the feet from under him.

That was what was about to happen to Police Sergeant Hamish Macbeth. But on a particularly fine sunny day when the mountains of Sutherland in the northwest of Scotland stood up blue against the even bluer sky and not a ripple moved on the surface of the sea loch in front of the village of Lochdubh, he was blissfully unaware of what the fates had in store for him.

The only irritation in his life was the appointment

of a constable to assist him, police headquarters in Strathbane having discovered that the small police station in Lochdubh was an excellent way of getting rid of the deadbeats. Constable Dick Fraser was marking time until his retirement. He was a lazy grey-haired man, but he had an amiable disposition, and since he'd arrived in Lochdubh a month ago there had been no crime at all, which suited him very well.

Hamish learned that there was a relative newcomer, an elderly widow called Mrs. Colchester, who had bought an old hunting box some miles outside Braikie. During the winter, he had meant to call on her, but somehow the days and months had slipped past.

Dick was asleep in a deck chair in the front garden, his breath causing his grey moustache to rise and fall.

"Get up!" snapped Hamish.

Dick's pale blue eyes slowly opened. He struggled out of the chair and stood up. Most of his weight was concentrated on a beer belly. He was quite short for a policeman, dwarfed by Hamish, who was over six feet tall.

"What's up?" he asked sleepily.

"We're going to call on a newcomer, a Mrs. Colchester."

"Someone killed the old bitch?" asked Dick.

"Why do you say that?"

"I heard gossip she's considered poison. Bad, nasty mouth on her and she's got two grandchildren from hell living with her. Also, she's right fed up because Lord Growther, who used to own the place, left Buchan's Wood, the prettiest part of the estate, to the town of Braikie. Now some lass on Braikie council has been appointed the council director of tourism and the environment and she's been running tours to the wood. She's renamed it the Fairy Glen."

"Where on earth did you pick up all this gossip?" marvelled Hamish. "You hardly move."

"When you're out, people stop by the hedge for a wee chat. It does not, surely, take the two of us to go there."

"Oh, yes it does, you lazy moron. Brush down your uniform. It's covered in biscuit crumbs. Let's get moving."

The house which Mrs. Colchester had bought lay six miles to the north of Braikie. It was an unprepossessing place at the end of a long drive, being built of grey granite without any creepers to soften its harsh square structure.

The doorbell was an old-fashioned one set into the stone. Hamish rang it. They waited a long time until they heard shuffling footsteps approach from the other side of the door. The woman who answered it was squat and bent, leaning on two sticks and peering up at them out of sharp black eyes from under a heavy fringe of wiry grey hair.

"Mrs. Colchester?" asked Hamish.

"Yes, what is it? Is it those grandchildren of mine again?"

"No, no," said Hamish soothingly, removing his peaked cap and nudging Dick to do the same. "Just a wee social call."

"You may as well come in. But make it short." Her accent had been anglicised but still held some lilting traces of the Highlands. Somewhere in the Hebrides, guessed Hamish.

She led them into a large square hall patterned with black-and-white tiles. It was wood-panelled. There was a hard chair by the door and a side table against one wall. Apart from those items, there wasn't any other furniture, and no paintings decorated the walls.

"Drawing room's on the first floor," said Mrs. Colchester. She waddled across the hall to where a stair lift had been built. She climbed in, fastened a seat belt, and said, "Follow me."

The stair lift went on and up, smoothly and efficiently, stopping on the first floor landing. Light flooded down from a blue glass cupola up on the roof. She extricated herself from the lift and led them into a large drawing room.

Hamish looked around, wondering if she had bought the furnishings along with the house. There were several grimy landscapes of Scottish scenes decorating the walls. The furniture was Victorian, heavy, solid, and intricately carved. A large silver-framed mirror dominated the marble mantelpiece. There were several round tables, dotted here and there, small islands on a sea of rose-patterned carpet, bleached pale by the sunlight.

From the window, Hamish could see Buchan's Wood. A tour bus drove up to a newly built clearing which served as a car park and began to dislodge passengers. He swung round.

"I believe you are upset that Buchan's Wood, or the Fairy Glen as I understand it has been renamed, is not a part of your estate."

"Oh, sit down and stop poking about," said Mrs. Colchester. "Do you dye your hair?"

Hamish's hair was flaming red in a patch of sunlight. "No," he said crossly.

"Well, as to your question, I was upset at first but then that Mary Leinster called on me. She persuaded me that the beauty of the place should be shown to as many people as possible. She has the second sight, you know."

"A lot of people claim to have that gift," said Hamish cautiously.

"Oh, but she is the real thing. I have my two grandchildren staying with me for the school holidays. Charles is twelve and Olivia sixteen. Mary called on me last week and said Charles was in peril because he was going to fall into the pool below the falls. I know he can't swim. I didn't believe her but two days later Charles did fall in and, if it hadn't been for one of the tourists who dived in and rescued him, he would have been drowned."

"I think we'll take a look at the place," said Hamish.

"Go ahead. Are you as stupid as you look?"

Hamish blinked. Then he rallied and said, "Are you as rude and nasty as you appear?"

"Get out of here," she snapped, "and take that fat fool with you. And don't come back."

"After such a warm welcome," said Hamish sweetly, "it will be right hard for me to stay away. Come along, Dick."

As they walked down the stairs to the hall, they found two children at the bottom of the stairs surveying them.

"I gather you must be Charles and Olivia," said Hamish.

"Cut the crap," said Charles. "Is the old bat dead yet?"

"She is very much alive," said Hamish coldly.

"Christ, she'll live forever," said Olivia gloomily.

Hamish sat down on the bottom step and surveyed them curiously. Charles was small and thin with a shock of fair, almost white hair and flat grey eyes. His sister was a slightly taller version with the same colour of hair and eyes. Both had very white skin and thin pale lips and long thin noses.

"Why do you want your grandmother dead?" he asked.

"Because our parents say our school fees are too much and they are threatening to send us to the local comprehensive where we'll be stuck with morons and chavs. If Granny dies, they get the money."

"You're English?"

"Yeah, from London," said Olivia. "You know, where real people live, instead of, like, moronsville up here."

The floorboards above them creaked. "Here she comes," said Charles. Both children scampered out the open door and disappeared down the drive.

"Let's go," urged Hamish. "A little o' Granny Colchester goes a long way."

"I'm hungry," complained Dick. "She could at least have offered us something."

"That old cow? Forget it. Let's have a look at this wood."

Groaning, Dick heaved his bulk into the passenger seat of the police Land Rover. "You'll need to feed your beasties anyway," said Dick. Hamish had two pets, a mongrel called Lugs and a wild cat called Sonsie. He had left them behind at the police station. To Hamish's relief, both animals seemed fond of Dick.

"Just a quick look," said Hamish, "and then I'd like to visit this Mary Leinster. I mean, think how easy it would be to get someone to shove that child in the pool and then get a friend on hand to save the boy. Second sight confirmed. No more arguments about the use of the wood from Granny."

They parked beside the tour bus. Hamish noticed that what looked like a gift shop was under construction. Mrs. Timoty, an old-age pensioner from Braikie, stood at the entrance to the wood beside a turnstile. "That'll be three pounds each," she said, "and five pounds for the car."

"This is police business," said Hamish, walking past her. They followed a pokerwork sign with the legend FAIRY GLEN.

Sutherland's frequent Atlantic gales leave the landscape dotted with poor bent-over apologies for trees, like men with their jackets blown up about their ears. But there are a few beautiful glens and waterfalls, sheltered from the brutality of the wind.

Because of the proximity of the Gulf Stream, former Scottish gardeners had been able to plant rare varieties of trees and shrubs. A gravelled path twisted its way among the beauty of overhanging trees and great bushes of fuchsia. They stood aside to let the tourists make their way back to their bus.

Hamish, followed by Dick, came to a rustic bridge spanning the pool. The roar of the waterfall, which descended into the pool, filled their ears, and little rainbows danced in shafts of sunlight.

"My, but it's rare bonnie," said Dick.

"Shh!" said Hamish. "Look at that!"

A kingfisher dived into the pool and rose again, a fish in its beak, its sapphire-blue wings flashing. It flew under the trailing branches of a weeping willow and disappeared.

Large flat grey stones surrounded the pool. Hamish guessed the boy must have been playing on one of them when he was pushed in. If he had been on the bridge with the sightseers, then someone would have noticed. The boy would need to have been lifted bodily over the railing.

Hamish had a longing just to stay there, drinking in the peace of the place. But he was becoming curious about this Mary Leinster.

"I think we should go to the town hall in Braikie and visit Miss Leinster," he said. "Did the gossips tell you how Mrs. Colchester got her money?"

"Herself was married to a merchant banker. Before his death, he sold the place to an American bank and she copped the lot on his death. So the daughter and son-in-law, that would be a Mr. and Mrs. Palfour, are right cheesed off because they're finding it hard to make ends meet. He's a landscape gardener and owns a nursery, but it's this recession. No one seems to want their gardens landscaped. The kids go to a progressive private school, you know, the kind where they're allowed to express themselves, which translates into a lot of four-letter words and no work."

Hamish looked at his sidekick with new respect. He knew how valuable gossip was in any investigation. He laughed. "Maybe you're like Poirot, Dick, and sit in your deck chair and exercise your little grey cells. How did you hear this?"

"Mrs. McColl, her what is married to that crofter up the brae at Lochdubh, goes out cleaning, and twice a week she and Bertha Dunglass goes up to the house. When Granny gets a letter from her daughter, she reads it aloud and laughs her nasty auld head off."

A cloud passed over the sun. The pool below them grew dark, mirroring the flying clouds overheard. Although it was a windy day, the glen was sheltered.

"Let's go," said Hamish.

Braikie was not very large and would have been considered a fair-size village in England. The locals did refer to it as "the village," feeling that sounded, well, *classier*.

The town hall was a massive red sandstone building. Mary Leinster had secured an office on the ground floor. They were told she was out but was expected back at any moment. They took seats in the reception area and settled down to wait.

Dick promptly fell asleep. The rumblings of his stomach and his gentle snores sounded out a little symphony.

A small woman walked into the reception area and

spoke to the receptionist at the desk and then swung round. "Mr. Macbeth? You wanted to see me?"

Hamish nudged Dick awake and got to his feet. The sun pouring in the open doorway was in his eyes and he could not see her clearly.

"Come through to my office," she said. Her voice had a gentle highland lilt.

She entered a room to the left of the hall and ushered them in. Mary Leinster took her place behind a desk and waved them into two chairs in front of it.

Hamish looked at her in wonderment. She had a heart-shaped face and wide blue eyes fringed by heavy lashes. Her hair was long and curly, strawberry blonde, and rioted down to her shoulders. She was wearing a low-cut green blouse of some silky material which showed the tops of two round white breasts.

Mary looked at Hamish and gave a slow smile. She had pink curved lips.

Hamish experienced a sudden breathlessness.

"What has brought Sutherland's famous police officer to see me?" she asked.

Hamish pulled himself together. Dick was gaping at Mary, his mouth open. Hamish leaned across, shut Dick's mouth, and glared at him.

"It is about the boy, Charles Palfour," he said. "I believe you haff the second sight." Hamish's accent always became more sibilant when he was excited or upset.

"I don't know if I have or not," said Mary. "I just had this premonition. It came and went in a flash. I saw the boy struggling in the water. I have often seen him playing down on those stones by the pool. So I warned Mrs. Colchester that the boy was not to play there. She didn't believe me. So it happened, ten days ago, just as I had envisaged. Do you believe in the second sight, Mr. Macbeth?"

"Hamish, please."

"Hamish then. I feel we are going to be friends."

"We have a seer in the village of Lochdubh, Angus Macdonald, who claims to have the second sight. You must forgive me, Mary. You see, before I met you I thought it might be a stunt to promote the Fairy Glen."

She gave a charming giggle. "Hamish, the place is extremely popular already." Then she grew serious and leaned her arms on her desk. "With the recession, you know, there's not enough work up here. Because of the popularity of the glen, we have been able to give work to wardens, build a gift shop, and bring money into the economy of the region. Now you must excuse me. I have a meeting."

Hamish stood up. Dick had fallen asleep. Hamish surreptitiously kicked him on the leg, and he awoke with a jerk.

"Here is one of our brochures." Mary handed one to Hamish. On the cover was a very good colour photograph of the kingfisher, rising from the pool, sunlight flashing from the spray on its wings.

Hamish desperately wanted to see her again but she was now holding the door open. He said goodbye and walked sadly out to the police Land Rover. He didn't know anything about her. Had she been wearing a wedding ring? He could not remember.

As he moved off, he said, "I wonder if she's married."

The sleepy source of gossip next to him said, "Yes, she is."

"How do you know that?"

"Oh, a wee bittie talk here and there. Her husband is Tim Leinster. He and Mary's two brothers are builders. Not much work around these days but I suppose they got the contract to build the gift shop."

"Now, that would be right illegal if she's giving contracts out to the nearest and dearest."

"No, it was passed by the council. They're the only builders in Braikie."

"Then why haven't I heard of them?" howled Hamish.

"They only moved up here from Perth last year."

"Why?"

"I suppose they followed Mary when she got the job. Also, they've done a bit of work here and there since they arrived and everyone says they're reasonable and honest."

That's life, thought Hamish gloomily. Romance

walks in one minute and walks out the next. Why am I such a failure with women? He thought of how he had nearly proposed marriage to television presenter Elspeth Grant; how he had once been deeply in love with Priscilla Halburton-Smythe, daughter of the colonel who ran the Tommel Castle Hotel, and how he had been forced to end the engagement because of Priscilla's sexual coldness.

Was he turning out to be one of those sad sacks, always doomed to fall in love with the unattainable?

He mentally pulled himself together. He probably wouldn't see her again.

When he got back to the police station, it was to find an angry message from police headquarters telling him to go directly to Cnothan where two stolen cars had been reported.

Hamish loaded the cat and dog into the back of the Land Rover. Dick was wide awake now and complaining bitterly of hunger.

On the road, they passed a tour bus with the legend FAIRY GLEN on the front. It seemed to be full of people. He reflected that Mary seemed to be a dab hand at publicity.

Hamish considered Cnothan a sour, unfriendly place, and although it was on his beat, he visited it as little as possible. One bleak main street led down to a man-made loch. The locals prided themselves on "keeping themselves to themselves."

He knew there was a caravan park and camping area outside the village and headed there. The missing cars were a blue Ford Fiesta and a Peugeot. He checked with the slatternly woman who ran the campsite to check for recent arrivals. She said there were just two, brothers, Angus and Harry McAndrews. Their tent was pitched out at the edge of the campsite.

The two men were seated outside their tent, cooking sausages on a frying pan over a camp stove. They were both skinheads, covered in prison tattoos.

"Whit does the filth want wi' us?" demanded one of them.

"I'm looking for two stolen cars," said Hamish.

"Whit's that got tae dae wi' us?"

Hamish looked around. Next to the brothers' tent was a large bell tent with the front flap tightly closed.

"What's in there?" he asked.

"Naethin' tae dae wi' us," said the one who seemed to be the elder.

"Then you won't mind if I have a look."

They both stood up. One reached down and picked up a tyre iron. "Get lost, copper," he snarled.

Hamish reached out, seized the arm holding the tyre iron, and twisted it hard. The man let out a yelp of pain and dropped it. His brother tried to run but Dick stuck out a foot and tripped him up. They cuffed both of them. Hamish then looked in the bell tent and found the cars. He charged both of them with theft. He phoned headquarters in Strathbane and was told to stay on guard until a police van arrived to take them away. To make sure the brothers did not try to escape, even though they were handcuffed, Hamish forced them down on the ground and dragged their trousers around their ankles.

He turned round to tell Dick to put the stove out only to find that Dick had served himself sausages on a paper plate and was busily eating them.

"You're a disgrace," complained Hamish.

"It's not as if they're evidence," said Dick through a mouthful of sausages. "These are rare good. I wonder if they got them locally?"

Back at the police station after what seemed like a long day and having completed all the necessary paperwork, Hamish retreated to the kitchen. From the living room came the noisy sounds of a television game show. He put his head around the living room door and shouted, "Mince and tatties for supper?"

Dick reluctantly lowered the sound, the remote control clutched firmly in one chubby hand. "What's that?"

"I asked you if you wanted mince and tatties for your supper?"

"Oh, aye, grand," said Dick.

"I'll call you when it's ready."

Dick threw him a pleading look. "Could I no' just eat my meal in here in front o' the telly? Just the once?"

Hamish thought wryly that Dick looked like a child pleading with a stern parent. "Oh, all right. But don't you start dropping food on the floor!"

Dick smiled and blasted up the sound again.

It wasn't as if the man was deaf, grumbled Hamish to himself. It was almost as if by jacking up the sound, he could be part of the show itself. "I've spoiled him," said Hamish to Lugs and Sonsie. "I've been happy just to go on as if I'm still on my own. But tomorrow, no more deck chair for Dick. He can come out on the rounds with me. Also, he'd better begin to do his share of the cooking."

He knew Dick was a widower whose wife had died ten years ago. He seemed to have no idea at all of household work and had even on one occasion plaintively asked Hamish to show him how the vacuum cleaner worked.

But the man was pleasant enough, and it didn't look as if any major crime was ever going to happen again.

The morning would prove Hamish wrong.

He was frying up bacon and eggs while Dick watched a breakfast show on television when the phone in the office rang.

When he answered it, Mary Leinster gasped out, "It's me. Mary. Come quickly. They've hanged him! In the glen," and rang off.

Hamish erupted into the living room and yelled, "Turn that damn thing off. We've got a murder!"

VISIT US ONLINE AT

WWW.HACHETTEBOOKGROUP.COM

FEATURES:

OPENBOOK BROWSE AND SEARCH EXCERPTS

•

AUDIOBOOK EXCERPTS AND PODCASTS

•

AUTHOR ARTICLES AND INTERVIEWS

•

BESTSELLER AND PUBLISHING GROUP NEWS

•

SIGN UP FOR E-NEWSLETTERS

•

AUTHOR APPEARANCES AND TOUR INFORMATION

•

SOCIAL MEDIA FEEDS AND WIDGETS

•

DOWNLOAD FREE APPS

Bookmark Hachette Book Group
@ www.HachetteBookGroup.com